MEKHTI

MEKHTI

Amy Bassan

Black Heron Press
Post Office Box 95676
Seattle, Washington 98145
www.blackheronpress.com

ISBN 0-930773-71-3

Black Heron Press
Post Office Box 95676
Seattle, Washington 98145
www.blackheronpress.com

One

He was married but his wife was in New York. She was pregnant and was on bed rest so she went back to her family there, to her parents and sisters and brothers and aunts and cousins who would take care of her. That was how I imagined them. Bringing her breakfast in bed, and little trays of cookies with nuts and sugar, and giving her daily reports. Who did what back home, who got a visa to come to America, who got married or engaged, who got arrested and thrown into jail. Probably they all put their hands and heads to her stomach and listened and told her what a beautiful baby it would be and what a wonderful husband she had, so kind and thoughtful to let her go back to her family at such a difficult time. I can only wonder what they told her, what they said he was doing all those months alone. What he told her when he called her over the phone, because he would never call while I was there. He was always very careful that I should never hear a word spoken to her.

Right away, I think it was only two or three weeks after I met him, he told me the story of how she tried to kill herself over him back when they were still in high school and just dating. How they had some trivial

argument and he walked out on her and later the call
came that she was in the hospital, she had swallowed a
whole bottle of sleeping pills. Her parents had found
her on the floor of her room passed out and had called
an ambulance. You see, he said to end the story, my
wife really loves me. My greatest fear is that she will do
it again and I will do anything to keep that from
happening.

After I heard the story I thought of her as a very
weak person, a little mouse, sitting at home biting her
nails and pacing the rooms while he was out at bars and
restaurants. I thought of her as the kind of woman who
is proud to catch a man, who considers it some kind of
accomplishment or even a stroke of luck. Who sits at
home all day or visits her friends and family because it
wouldn't be respectable or proper for her to get a job.
Who can't go shopping without his telling her what to
buy. Who probably can't even finish a sentence without
looking his way. At night she lies awake in his arms and
thinks how lucky she is to have him, to have him
making all the decisions for her and bringing her money
and children. Without him she would have nothing.
And she turns toward him with her arms around him
and falls asleep, knowing she will always have her new
life and him.

My wife is very jealous, he said to me more than

once. He tells me once out of the blue she stepped into the shower behind him and thrust a kitchen knife under his chin. And said, If you ever cheat on me, I'll slit your throat.

He says, My wife is a very strong woman. But I can't imagine it. All I see is the girl who has been petted all her life, an Eastern princess who didn't even know how to cook until she moved into her married home. Who is now in New York being served hand and foot by an army of devoted kinswomen and being reassured of her husband's good will and fidelity. A tiny, frail, dark-haired mouse of a woman.

There was a time close to the end when he came to me with red red eyes and hands practically trembling. He'd had a dream, he said, a dream of his wife and black clouds that wept blood. She's going to die, he said, jumping up in the tiny room and pacing. It will kill her, I know it. I have to be there, he said. I have to go to her when she goes into labor. And like a good friend I held his head and stroked his hair and said, She'll be all right, but go to her. You should be there when your child is born. And two days later they called him, said she was beginning the first contractions. He bought a ticket and flew to New York, stopping only to call me from the airport and say he didn't know when he would be back. He was gone for five days.

Secretly I was hoping she'd die, and the baby too. Or that the baby would live. Then he would take it back with him and I could raise it. But she had to die. Those five days I walked around in a pink haze of rage. Die die die, I chanted. I drank pennyroyal tea so that she would miscarry. I jumped from high places. I pummeled my stomach. I cut my arms, wincing and wishing the pain was hers. Wishing hurting her could be as easy as hurting myself. But through all my witchcraft she survived and had a baby girl.

He never called me. I heard only when he got back. I heard how healthy the baby was, how perfect, born with black hair and eyes and perfect tiny ears and even little fingernails. I heard how brave she had been and how she never once screamed. I was the one who felt like screaming, because all this time I had thought once the baby is born, she will come home, and it will all come to an end. Countless times I had clung to him and asked, What will happen when she comes back? What will happen to us? But it was a question neither of us could answer. We couldn't imagine things going back the way they were, being apart. But we both knew she had to come back and things would be very different then. Could he see me at all? Once or twice a week? A month? I couldn't imagine it being less than once a day. I couldn't imagine not hearing his voice, not confiding

in him every day, listening to him work out solutions to
my other, trivial problems.

Almost every night I slept over at his apartment. I
still wasn't old enough to get my license so I took the
bus, forty-five minutes each way. Every morning he
cooked me breakfast (although no doubt if it were his
wife he slept with, she would have had to do the
cooking for both of them) and after he left I went
through his closets and drawers, smelling his soap, his
clothes, his food, all the things that went into his smell.
His sweaty shirts, his cigarettes, his pillow. My own
arms and hair smelled like him.

The days I did go to school and did not stay in his
apartment (lounging on the couch watching cartoons
and soap operas, six years old again and home sick
from school) I sat in a classroom staring into space,
smelling the ends of my hair and my fingertips. My
grades dropped from A's to C's because I didn't do my
homework and missed a lot of tests but nobody ever
noticed. Teachers noticed, but you can't count them.
They noticed the circles under my eyes, the clothes I
wore two and three days in a row. They noticed that
smell (the smell was from the apartment, not from me,
because I never smoked pot) and I could tell they
wanted to ask if I'd been doing drugs.

The other kids' attitudes changed toward me too. Before I'd been someone completely different, preppy, with all the answers. People had been afraid to talk to me because it was rumored I was stuck up. Anyway what was there to talk about with someone like me? You could talk about pointillism in art, about the Ottoman Empire or the Warsaw pact, but I didn't know anything about X-files or MTV.

Now they were afraid of me because I was scary. I was a zombie, a druggie. I slept through my classes with my eyes open and if you talked to me I just stared through you. Maybe I really was stoned all the time. Maybe just breathing his breath was enough. But more likely it was my life that had brainwashed me. Living like that, in love, in fear, in hate. Counting down the months, the days, until whatever came sooner—his wife's homecoming or my graduation—when I would leave for college and finally reclaim myself.

At school, surrounded by young voices and faces, I heard his voice, his man's voice, smoker's voice, foreigner's voice, pervert's voice in my ear. Like the devil on your shoulder or the voice of your conscience that people in those '50s movies always went crazy trying to shut up.

I had been going to that school for two years only and

had no friends, none of the teachers knew me well. There was just one teacher, the Honors English teacher who had had me in her class for two years. She pulled me aside once as I was leaving class, saying she wanted to have a talk with me. She was a good teacher, young but cynical in a way that always made students laugh, and back when I still cared I always felt that she made me work too hard. Graded me more like I was in college than in high school, gave me B's where an average student would have gotten A-pluses.

After all the other students had filed out she shut the door behind them and locked it and sat down on top of her desk. She began by saying, I've noticed your work has really been slipping. You don't seem to care anymore. This isn't like you not to care about school. Then she began talking about my potential. That, if nothing else, woke me from my stupor. Maybe she'd been saving it as a secret weapon against my apathy, a last throw of the rope that could pull me to safety. I loved to hear anyone rave about me. She said, In the ten years I've been a teacher you are the brightest English student I have ever had and had I not heard the same thing from your teachers in every other subject I would not have believed it. Everything you have done this year, you have done better than any tenth grader anyone in this school has ever seen. Up until two months ago. You've been given a great gift, she said, looking into my eyes

even though I tried to look away. You aren't allowed to
throw it away. Think, if not of yourself, then of others,
what amazing things a person like you can do for
society. Right now you should be using all your energy
to cultivate these tremendous talents. It's your responsibility. I don't know what you've been doing when
you're not at school, she said, all the while giving me a
look that said she had a pretty good idea what I'd been
doing, but right now you need to concentrate on acting
your age. On being young, on learning and growing.

She kept repeating the part about it being my responsibility to cultivate my mind and that my job was to stay
in school. She left me weak-kneed and red in the face,
close to tears because I was so grateful for her praise
and so angry that it had come so late. What good was
kindness now? I was so hungry for it, but for the past
few months it was like my stomach was stapled, my lips
sewn shut. Eventually she let me go, never once asking
me directly what it was that had made me change, but
I could tell she was hoping I would confide in her, if not
this time then later.

After that day ended I could not go back. I could not
go home either. Any place I went would suck me in and
make me a part of it. A part of school, a part of my
family, a part of him. As long as I stayed outside,
walking, I would keep myself whole. So I walked and

walked and when it got too cold I went into the library downtown and read until closing. Eventually I let myself into the house after everyone had gone to bed and fell asleep in my own room.

I thought about my tremendous talents, my amazing gifts. What ability? What gifts? If I really were so gifted, with such a bright future, wouldn't I be happier? If I really were so intelligent, wouldn't I be wiser? Capable of making better choices? And as for my accomplishments, I had none, never having finished anything I started. All my endeavors, drawing, writing, music lessons, ballet, figure skating, all the other lessons over all the years—in all of them I was clearly mediocre, too disappointed in myself to continue. My only true accomplishment was a thing no one even knew about. And you can say it was what was responsible for the breaking of my life.

Although my father somewhere, in some other place, wherever he ran to, is from Iran, and although as a child I have memories of grandmas and aunties talking to me in Persian, and although my mother says that by two years old I was babbling back, I forgot it all when those happy times (times of big families and love between adults and children) ended, when we came back to the US. My greatest accomplishment was teaching myself, starting in the eighth grade with books and tapes in the library, to speak Persian. An archaic Persian that no one uses anymore, not even the modern Persian that I am supposed to have known from birth. Were it not for that I would never have met him. It never would have turned out this way.

Does anyone know how it would have been? Would I have been valedictorian of my class and gone from there to an expensive East Coast college where students sat under the oaks pulling apart difficult philosophical issues? Then maybe Harvard medical school, my ninth-grade dream? Would I have held onto my nice high school boyfriend, a nerd like me who gave me flowers on my birthday and wanted so badly for me to say I loved him? He'll never understand why I suddenly wanted us to sleep together and then just as suddenly dumped him. He thinks I am a monster, a predator, a user. He doesn't understand who is what. Who told me to sleep with my high school boyfriend and then said, If you had been a virgin I would have had no right to touch you, not as a married man.

A little less potential would have been better in the long run. A little more normalcy. Not to be curious. Not to have learned that language.

He was standing in the doorway at the class Christmas party. I was an ESL volunteer. It was ten days until

Christmas. I asked, Do you want to come in? He didn't
understand. I pointed inside. He held up his cigarette.
I asked in Persian, Do you speak Persian? His face
brightened. God grant that someday I will learn to
speak your language as well as you speak mine. He
rambled, repeating himself. God grant, God willing.
Amanda, the other volunteer, warned that they had
been drinking, but I couldn't believe it. I didn't see any
bottles. And Muslims weren't supposed to drink. But
these were not Muslims. And when he said, It would be
interesting to practice English with an American girl
like you, I gave him my phone number without hesita-
tion. I remember running down the hall in search of a
yellow sticky pad. I kept the paper he gave me with his
number on it for I don't know how long afterward.
Until it got lost. The awkward English printing and
funny European style numbers, 7's with hooks and
crossed like t's. Proof that there was a beginning.

Just a quiet, dark man in a worn gray suit. What harm
could he do? Could you ever have anticipated the
strong arms, the sweat smell of his armpits, his hot
saliva and his tender fingertips in your hair? The violence and the gentleness of it all mixed up. Could you
ever have anticipated the hold he would have on you?
So that when you woke up he was the first thing on
your mind, he was all you wanted. No food, no drink,
only him.

Two

I told him that my mother's father was Jewish and he
said, You're one of us. One of us in more ways than one.
But who I was was not easy to find out. I tried asking my
mother about it. Not that I hadn't asked before. Especially when I was little, those first three or four years
after we came back. I asked her about my grandmother
and the aunties and about other things, things I don't
remember now. Younger cousins, a baby I liked to play
with. A pair of finches in a cage, they used to hang in the
courtyard in summer. A special kind of butter cookie I
liked that only the women in my father's house knew
how to make. I never tasted it after I came here.

I used to talk a lot about grandma and the aunties
and write them letters and send them with my draw-
ings. If we baked cookies I would put some aside in a
little plastic bag and say, These are for the aunties when
we go back to Tehran. I would spend all day in school
on an art project to give them, macaroni collages or
paper plate Thanksgiving turkeys. I probably thought
my mother would mail it somehow. I made up games
around them, games where I was traveling to their
house, where I was flying a plane or sailing a ship to
them. When I got to a hard part on my journey I would

call them on my Sesame Street phone from my Sesame Street playhouse and they would counsel me. They always gave me good advice. Jump over that poisonous snake, they would say, or don't talk to that magic puppy, it's really a witch in disguise. And I would tramp around the house in circles pretending I was getting closer and closer.

My mother didn't like it that I missed them so much, but she tried not to show it. She would simply say, I don't know when we're going back. I don't know.

The war when it started between Iran and Iraq gave me terrible nightmares. I didn't know what a war was but I imagined terrible men, like pirates or headless horsemen, rushing into the house at night, pulling everyone from their beds and slitting their throats. I saw blood everywhere and refused to wear anything red. I wouldn't let anyone sleep in bed with me, not my cat, not my friends for sleepovers, not even my mother because I was afraid those same men would burst into my room and slit their throats too. I dreaded waking up and finding severed body parts, my pillow drenched with blood.

It didn't matter that we got no letters, no phone calls from my father or his family. I had no concept of distance. They were right there with me, no more separating us than a thin wall or a few city blocks. At any time my mother and I would hop on a plane, step out into the airport in Tehran and we would be reunited. You just had to feel that way, having felt a love like theirs. The aunties holding me up to look at the pretty finches, the flowers in the courtyard, my grandma holding me on her lap, telling me stories, brushing my hair. I remember the softness of her clothes, her spicy smell. But unlike the aunties her kindness was ephemeral. One minute she was hugging me to her, the next minute she was chasing me around the room for having pinched her or stolen something from her room.

My memories of them are all disappearing. Two, three years after we left I could remember day by day, as clear and sunlit as the courtyard. Now it's just little winks and muted flashes, like a shiny fish through dark water. Some mornings I wake up and something new pops into my head, and I know I have been dreaming about them. After I forgot all the words I knew, I could no longer remember the sounds of their voices. It would just be my voice, speaking over their picture memories.

Sometimes when I was little my mom would speak Persian with me. But only when she was in a special mood. If we were in the grocery store she would nudge me and say that somebody had funny hair or wore too much makeup. Her funny voice, the mistakes she made always made me laugh. Back in Tehran I knew she was different from my father, that she was an American, because my grandmother and aunts and uncles were always talking about it. But it wasn't until I came here that I realized why her Persian sounded so odd and why she spoke English more than anyone else and why my grandma and aunts didn't speak it at all. Tehran was my whole world, and when I came here and found out that everyone spoke English like my mother I was amazed. Until then I had thought it was a private language she had invented just for the two of us.

When my mother remarried the first time things really began to change. Persian we had long ago forgotten, the aunties and uncles and grandma and cousins were barely real people to me, and now that we were a new family there was no point in remembering my old father anymore. I was old enough and young enough that I didn't really care. By then I knew he was never coming back. I did everything I could to please my new dad, which meant hiding all the parts of me that weren't American. I had long stopped asking my mother questions. There were no photographs, nothing in the house from Tehran. No physical evidence at all. Not even in me. My brown hair and pink skin could have belonged to anyone's kid. If I ever saw a person from the Middle East with black hair, olive skin, almond eyes, a little shiver went through me and a wall came up between

me and him: foreigner. But when Mekhti spoke to me of
his mother and father (he often talked about his father,
who died two years before to the day we met) I began
to miss my family again. Again I would wake up in the
morning with the scent of their house in my nose. While
I was still living at home, while I was still me, individual, separate.

Why did they never try to contact me, I wondered.
Could they still be thinking about me all this time?
Their grandchild, their brother's daughter, son's daughter. I pictured my grandmother as a gray-haired old
woman in black since I had forgotten what she looked
like, forgotten that she was fat instead of thin, I pictured her sitting in the courtyard in the sun thinking of
me. Sad that I had been snatched from her so suddenly.
I imagined my aunties dressing their own daughters,
cooking them meals, sending them to school, even arranging their weddings, I imagined them imagining
me, guessing what I looked like at six, ten, fourteen.
Worrying that there was no one to look after me the
same way they looked after my cousins.

It's funny but I was so afraid to broach the subject
with my mother. I made up all kinds of conditions for
myself that would make it more difficult for me to
initiate the conversation with her. She must be alone, it
must be a weekend before bed, she must not be tired,

she must be in a good mood. My stepdad must be out of the house. But eventually there was a day when she had a half-day off from work and I was still at home on Christmas vacation and we were talking to each other in and out of the kitchen, almost like old times, and I sat down across from her at the kitchen table and asked her why she had never written to my grandmother after we left. And when she had given her answer I asked her why she had never let my father come to see me. I listened to her answer and then I asked another question. And another. We got angrier and angrier, me flinging questions at her and she trying to defend herself with answers that were really excuses, so that we ended up screaming at each other and slamming doors, she the front door and me the door to my room.

She said she left because of the war and because life there was unbearable for a Western woman. That she never realized my father was the problem until he followed us back to the States and the terrible arguing, her depression, continued. I remember that time, but just barely. Although I have no memories of my father in Tehran, I remember him in California. I remember them arguing through the night in the tiny apartment, I remember my father's hands on my shoulders and then gone, and I never saw him again. We moved to another state. My mother said, And I never spoke to any of them again because I was so afraid they would try to

take you from me, take you back there. You were an
Iranian citizen, after all. And in the eyes of the Iranian
government I would have no rights at all and Ali, every
right. But grandma, I said, but my aunties. My mother's
eyes looked like she wanted to cry. I know you missed
them terribly when we left and it hurt me to hear you
talk about them all the time. All the little things you
used to make them, then give to me to save for when we
went back. But even if I had wanted to get in touch with
them, how could I? I couldn't read or write Persian. I
couldn't write to them, and it's impossible to place an
overseas call there. And then when the war began, well,
who knows what happened then? Your father, if he
really did go back there, maybe he became a soldier.
Maybe he's dead. Who knows? It's not like he ever tried
to keep in touch. He didn't want to see you. He didn't
want to find out what happened to you. When we
separated and I sent the papers asking for full custody,
he just sent them back, signed, he never even tried to
contest it.

This was something I had heard my whole life, my
mother's story of how my father had relinquished all
parental rights. He left me, he didn't care what happened to me, he didn't want anything to do with me.
One minute she was saying how fearful she was that
they, the family, would come after me, the next she was
complaining that he had never tried to locate me, that

he never made the effort. Who would want a father like that, she liked to say, especially when Don and his family had always been so kind to me and treated me like their own daughter? But if that were true, then why did being with her and Don make me feel even more alone?

I began to resent my mother. She was like a brick wall standing in the way of my finding my father, my grandmother and aunts. Only she knew the secret to finding them, but she of all people was fighting me for it. Mekhti asked me how did it go with my mother and I told him about our conversation in the kitchen. I asked him how I could ever possibly find them without her help. I didn't even know their full names. But he didn't know how to do it either. He had never been to Iran. Going about it completely alone, all I could think to do was call the Iranian embassy in Canada. But it was a long distance call that my mother would find out about just by looking at the phone bill. I didn't want her to know. She said, Please don't do any of this in Don's house. He would be so hurt. So I went to the house of a girl from school, a girl I really didn't know that well (not well enough to go to her house) and made the call from there. I told her I would pay her back, she said not to worry about it. She said her mother made calls to friends in Canada all the time and she would never even notice it. I dialed the number and a woman an-

swered saying something in Persian. For a second the
words rose inside me, for a second I thought I would be
able to remember what to say back to her. But instead I
asked, Could you speak English please? She had a deep
voice and a thick foreign accent. I told her that I was an
Iranian citizen by birth and that I was trying to locate
my family in Tehran. She said Just a minute please and
for a long time there was just silence. I guessed she
must be asking someone else in the office what to do
about me. When she came back on the line she asked,
What are their names please? When I told her my
father's last name and told her I only knew the first
names of the aunts she just made a laughing sound like
blowing air through her nose and said, That name is as
common as Jones or Smith here. You'll never be able to
find them that way. Do you remember their address?
No, I told her. It was just a big house with a courtyard
and windows with a kind of lattice on them. Maybe you
could find it. I'll see, the lady said, just a minute. Then
a man came on the line. Miss, he said, we have no way
to help in finding lost relatives. I suggest you ask your
family for information. Iran is a very isolated country
and it is nearly impossible to find anything out from
here. Even international aid organizations like the Red
Cross have been unsuccessful in reuniting war survi-
vors with overseas relatives. But perhaps someday you
will be able to make a trip there, okay? Perhaps you will
return to your old neighborhood in Tehran and some-

one there will remember your papa. Good luck, okay? I'm sorry no one here could assist you.

And that was that. He seemed like a nice person, like he wanted to help. But go to Iran? That was impossible, for the next few years at least. Not until I turned eighteen. The girl whose phone it was suggested I call information in Los Angeles and look up my father's name in the directory. But when I gave the operator my father's name she came up with fourteen different listings. How was I ever to find out if one of them was my father? What if none of them was? What if he had moved long ago, gone back to Tehran?

Three

What drew me to him in the beginning were his stories. They were like a finger that caught me and drew me in, down to him. I could be so angry at him, so unhappy, and he would just sit down beside me and begin to talk. His adventures in childhood, something that happened to him the day before, an interesting show he'd watched or maybe just a funny joke. And without fail his voice would overcome me, turn my head and warm my face so that I had to listen. Afterwards I felt exhausted but happy, like he had taken me with him on a dangerous trip and brought me back unscathed.

At first they were outlandish stories meant to entertain and amaze me. Wolves in Siberia, aliens in Atlantis, rats eating humans in wartime Stalingrad. Rats, you see, have a special chemical in their saliva that acts as a local anesthetic. And during the war, when the Germans had the city surrounded and everyone was starving and freezing, rats would creep into people's rooms at night and gnaw away at their faces as they slept. What with the cold, they couldn't feel a thing, and when they woke up the next morning parts of their ears and noses would be chewed off. People ate other people too, once people began to die of starvation. In the city of Samarkand some funny little bones were found in meat sold in the marketplace and they turned out to be human finger bones. There was also a law in Samarkand during the war that a person convicted of stealing bread would be sentenced to death by firing squad. So all over the city there were accusations, people with personal vendettas and scores to settle, and people who just wanted an extra share of rations and thought to get it by accusing their neighbor of stealing. Towards the end, men of sixty, seventy years were being called into service. Mekhti's grandfather hid in the cellar during a recruitment roundup, where soldiers searched every house in the city for men who were not contagious, not bedridden, older than twelve and younger than seventy-two years of age. That was the war.

And then there were stories about the golden days of Samarkand, about kings and queens, gold palaces and buried treasure. There was Timur who employed ten thousand men to bury his cache of gold in a spot where no one could ever find it, then had them and all of their families killed on the spot so that they could never give away the secret. And his wife, Bibi Khanim, who commissioned fantastic palaces to commemorate their love. Once her palaces were complete, she had the architect killed (some say he was in love with her) so that he would never again create anything so beautiful.

Bibi Khanim was sailing across a river with a man who was madly in love with her. When she got tired of his advances, she told him to lean over the side of the boat and take a drink from the water there. Then she told him to take a drink from the other side. She asked him if the water from either side tasted any different. He said no. She told him that it was the same with women. No matter what woman, they all tasted the same. After that he left her alone.

There is another story that she gave her admirer a basket of eggs dyed different colors and told him that all women were like the eggs, differently beautiful on the outside but the same on the inside. And another story where she held up her hand, and this is what Mekhti used to do to me, hold up his hand to me like someone saying Stop, then fold his fingers over and say that women are like that. Standing up, they are all different sizes. But lying down, they are all the same.

For me the Bibi Khanim stories were like riddles with no answer. Was he trying to tell me why he could, why he could not, choose between us? He didn't want to leave his wife for me because he was already married to her, and why trade one woman for another if they are all the same? But if it was me who wanted him more, why couldn't he stay with me? We were all the same to him, what difference did it make to him who he was with?

He told me stories of his adventures as a photographer among the city palaces, as a musician playing at weddings in mountain villages, an antique exporter and con man, a sergeant driving tanks across mine fields and leading convoys through icy mountain passes. I listened and listened. There was nothing I would not believe. But gradually his stories lost their humor. Life was not always happy. His father was arrested when Mekhti was in the sixth grade. His mother left for months at a time to petition the Soviet courts in Tashkent. He earned enough money to eat by catching pigeons and selling them in the marketplace.

That year he hardly ever went to school. Mondays the museums were closed, they became his own private palaces. He climbed up into the highest towers, the rafters where the pigeons roost, dragging big canvas sacks below him. Climbed the cool stone walls into spaces long neglected and forgotten, where caught spinning in a shaft of light is a whirlwind of dust a thousand years old. Where everything around you is ancient and crumbling and the modern city seen between stone pillars and blocks is hazy with heat. Where

you hear the cooing of birds, you sneak, you catch one
by the tail feathers and whoosh, a whole riot of bird
wings sweeps around your head, beating in your ears,
a bird whirlwind spinning out of the dust and spread-
ing out over the city and you watch them, you could
spend hours in these cool tower shadows, creeping
like a thief. No one knows you are here.

I used to lie on the bed and dream about that city, on
my own bed in my own house where I was alone.
Dream of the heat and the dust of the plains, the prayers
five times a day loud from the tops of the mosques, the
dirty crowded bazaar where you could find anything
for sale, the lonely mountain passes and villages as
secure as fortresses in their valleys. Of railway stations
where chic Russian girls mingled with Uzbek villagers
from the mountains and Muslim women veiled from
head to toe. Of the elaborate brick houses and the gypsy
quarter where every month or so there was a riot, thirty
wounded and one man dead with a hatchet in his head.

He walks me down streets of a bazaar where in
wartime they sell human meat. We kick up clouds of
dust, red, and in the distance are golden domes and
mud shacks. People on the street are swathed in dirty
sheets and towels up to their necks and their faces are
seamed and barbed, their eyes dulled by dirt. There
are girls who sway on high heels, girls in miniskirts

and red lipstick and switchblades. Men calling out a bargain, men drinking and smoking hashish, sitting on their heels in narrow alleyways, men ganging up and knifing each other in the back. This is his city and if I am correct he will say to me, You are a part of it. He will wrap his arms around my neck in a choke hold I can't escape. He will hold me until I am tired of his arms, until the weight of his arms and the feel of his clothes become second skin. Could it be? And around ten o'clock he will take me home. I will sleep all night in his bed, his. When he comes to me it won't hurt. There will be no ripping or tearing of meat. It will be clean and smooth. Natural. No enduring or forcing or pushing away or pulling back. His back under my fingers will turn smooth and lean. Like the time I smoked weed and suddenly wherever I looked at him or touched him he became more what I wanted and I was falling, falling into a soft bed. We will stroll his streets and I on his arm will say, Look who I am. Look who he's made me. I will listen to his voice as I fall asleep. My hands stretch and smooth his limbs and make them perfect, perfect. Who is perfect? I can't imagine.

Four

Alone in his apartment, I wandered around smelling things. I took olfactory inventory. Opened his closet and buried my nose in his shirts hanging, shook his cigarettes out of the carton and sniffed their sweetness. I stood a long time in his empty shower, still steamy because he had just used it that morning, and breathed in the knockout perfume scent of his shampoo. Wriggled my toes on the still-wet tiles. Staying in his apartment alone was like watching him asleep. His life was a still frame, ready for me to examine at my leisure. When it was sunny I spent a lot of time in the kitchen learning to cook. I bought an old book from the library book sale, used for fifty cents, and out of it practiced apple pie, glazed raisin chicken, bundt cake with chocolate swirl. When he came home at night he just shoved my messes into the refrigerator and forgot about them. I watched a lot of TV too. He had a big color TV, brand new, one of the first things I noticed when I first saw his apartment. And a VCR. I watched lots of taped cartoons, Disney movies from his four-year-old daughter.

Lying on the couch, the quilt wrapped around me, I would relax my body and slowly, painstakingly superimpose his body over mine. Slowly I could feel myself becoming him, filling his body, feeling what it would be like to be inside him as he breathed, listened, spoke, saw. The longer I stayed in his apartment, the more he would belong to me. The plants with rough edges, the Turkish carpet on the living room floor and the other on the wall, everything in his apartment would transfer bits of him to me. I liked to stretch out on his bed, our bed, when he was gone, scissor my feet under the covers (the dirty sheets were so soft and felt so good) and bury my face in his pillow. Sometimes I found his fine black hairs and I saved them.

I remember the first time I came to his apartment. It was the second or third time we met. He came to the corner lot at the edge of my neighborhood, as always, and I got in his car and we drove for a little while in the dark (it was only five or six o'clock but it gets dark early in December) and then he said he wanted to go someplace where we would be more comfortable. So we drove for a long time and I settled in for the ride. It was warm and steamy in the car, thick and dark all around, and the lights of the freeway reflected on the window glass.

Sometimes it seemed like we were always driving somewhere and the drives were always the same. They went on and on forever, always in the dark, always thick and warm with being together but lonely all the same, lonely and sad and scary as the freeway lights fled behind us. I never knew where we would end up.

We went over the bridge. Then there was an exit and a few turns where everything was dark and carless. We pulled up in front of some building. He let me in with a key and we walked up a flight of stairs and down a red corridor that had me panicked, thinking we had come to a hotel. Then in front of one door he stopped, opened it, and I understood. This was the apartment where he lived.

Everything was very plain. I couldn't picture his wife living here and I never could in all the days I lived there. You'd think I could have imagined her cooking dinner, watching TV, even sleeping in bed, it was after all her room too, but it was as if the apartment had swallowed up every trace of her presence there. There were blank walls everywhere, a TV table, shelves of cinder blocks, no furniture anyone could really care about. A cement balcony where later we would sit outside in the rain and he would smoke. He sat me down on the couch and turned on the TV. I'm going outside to have a smoke, he said. Make yourself comfortable. I wonder what he was thinking while he was smoking outside, whether he was planning what to do or say next, whether he was just letting his mind empty.

There was a documentary on TV about lions. When he came back in he sat down and watched it with me. I like shows like this, he said. Shows about nature. As we watched I thought about how we were like two lions meeting on the savanna the way we sat together. Testing how close to get to each other without making it dangerous, how much space to leave in between. That was the first night he played the keyboard for me and afterwards whenever I heard him playing those songs it gave me a certain feeling, the feeling of that night. All I had to do was listen and it was there.

Five

It was after the fight with my mother that I remembered the box, but I couldn't remember the last place I'd seen it. It must have been when I was nine or ten, before we even moved here. But I knew she still had it. I ran up the stairs to the bedroom, because her closet is where she keeps all the untouched boxes. Shoe boxes, liquor boxes full of old clothes and papers , plastic boxes, boxes jammed full of stuff she would rather forget. I hauled out the ones on the floor and dug through them. There were some on the top shelf too but too high for me to get them all down. I ran my hands inside each of them until at last I knew what I was touching. Something that felt like dried macaroni, something else that flaked off like scales when I touched it. When I took my hand away I saw the fingertips were covered in green and gold glitter. Inside my special box were all the things I'd saved for them. A poem I wrote that had been included in the school newsletter for parents. A piece of coral washed up on the beach. A snakeskin and three pieces of a robin's egg, bright blue. I held both of them in my hand, comparing the dry papery and brittle-sharp feelings. Before I knew it I had crumbled both in my hand.

Six

I think part of the reason my parents didn't try to keep me at home was because Don was having his own problems. One of his daughters, the youngest, was having trouble in college, flunking out over a boyfriend or something like that, and wanted to come home to stay. It was easier for them then with one less body at home. Most nights I spent there, in his apartment. He always went to sleep before I did, sleeping on his stomach with his face pressed sideways into the pillow. The quicker he fell asleep the harder it was for me. I would lie there, holding onto his arm, watching the darkness slowly expand around me and worrying. Worrying because I was so little and so many catastrophes were waiting to happen, so many forces could disrupt my unnatural, precarious happiness. I tried to picture her coming back but I stopped when I couldn't imagine how I would feel. My throat got tight and I couldn't go any farther. My life would end at that point in time when she came back, like a trail through the woods that suddenly ends in a cliff, a catastrophe, an avalanche, an explosion.

Seven

My mother had another marriage before this one. A bad marriage. It only lasted a year and a few months. What's strange is we've lived almost all our lives in different marriages with men, first with my father, then with Glen the bad stepfather, then with Don, but what it feels like and the way my mother will tell it is that we have always lived without men. Besides the memory of it being bad, my only clear memory of that marriage is at night, of climbing into bed between the two of them when they were watching TV and falling asleep on my stepfather's chest. At six years old that way my most heavenly experience, to fall asleep on a man's naked chest. I had almost forgotten. But later on, with Mekhti, I would remember at the times I lay my head on his chest, when I lay curled up beside him. He always said that was something people did only after sex, lay like that, and that was how I remembered suddenly.

Eight

I had two friends in high school. One was my boyfriend Jason and the other was Terecita, the girl that let
me come over to her house and make long distance
calls on her phone. I hardly knew her at all, but she was
in my English class and lately she had been coming to
sit beside me during lunch time. To me Terecita was
kind of dumb but very beautiful. She had long black
hair that was always covering her face, sliding over her
cheeks like a waterfall. But she was only beautiful
until she moved, because she had an annoying habit
of jiggling her foot when she sat in a chair and she
made sniffing noises all the time. I felt sorry for her
because she was so timid and shy, and she probably
felt sorry for me for the same reasons, plus I wasn't
pretty. That's a word you could never use for me. I felt
comfortable in masculine words only. If someone had
told me I was handsome I would have believed them,
but pretty, never.

Terecita liked to talk and she talked to me a lot since
I never knew what I should say to her. The strange thing
was how much we were really alike, even though we
were so different on the outside. Her parents were
divorced just like mine, and her father was from some

country in South America, Uruguay or Paraguay, I don't remember which, but it was supposed to be the wealthier of the two. But unlike me she went there to visit her father every other summer. She knew him, but she didn't really like him. Maybe I used Terecita to make myself feel superior. Because even though she had a father who was interested in seeing her and who paid for her to visit him every other summer, she and her mom lived their lives together in near poverty. My mother was always reminding me how lucky we were to own our own house, not to have to pay rent (although really it was Don's house) how we never had to worry about money, how I would never have to worry about paying for college. In contrast there was lonely Terecita, whose mother had to work because she hadn't remarried, who lived in a tiny rented house where there was never any food in the kitchen. They ate salads and things like tortillas with plain melted cheese on them night after night. Terecita's father was Catholic and he wouldn't divorce her mother, so they were just separated, but aside from the plane tickets he never sent any money. Since they were still married, no one could make him pay child support.

When my mother met Terecita she said she felt sorry for her mother and for Terecita too. That might have been us if I hadn't divorced him, she said. And she was always saying, Aren't we lucky to have Don?

My mother always made me believe we were some-how better than everyone else, even when we were living in apartments and eating on top of our cardboard moving boxes, she always made me believe our luck was better. She walked into expensive stores wearing flashy rings and designer jackets and no one could ever guess the rings were glass, the designer jackets knockoffs, no one could believe she was less than who she said she was. Tagging along behind her, I felt like I was the dead giveaway, dirty, sullen, bad-man-nered. She stopped taking me shopping with her when I was twelve or thirteen because she said I didn't do my hair, I didn't stand up straight enough, I wore holes in my jeans. But without her to take me places I didn't have anywhere to go. Riding in the car with her, my face pressed up against the glass, the streets out-side scared me.

Everything I did was ugly. Sometimes she would just come into my room and pick up a piece of clothing between her red nails and sniff it and say, Eew, this smells! And then she would smile at me and say, Don't you want some nice clothes?

The only good thing about Terecita's house was the brand new computer with an internet capability. Terecita understood, at least a little bit, how I felt about

my father and she let me use her computer to search for
him. We looked up his name in phone directories,
search engines, we got information on how to locate
missing persons in the U.S. and other countries. None
of it helped. And her house was always cold, because
heat was expensive.

Terecita, so slender and beautiful, lying still, like a
bird with its head under its wing. We would draw
together in her room, look at magazines, listen to the
radio. Sometimes I wondered what it would be like to
be a boy and fall in love with Terecita. Then I wondered
what would have happened if I had put her together
with Mekhti, if the same thing would have happened
that happened to me. Would she have reacted in the
same way, or would she have been stronger? Terecita,
stronger than me. I didn't tell her when it began, after
all we were on vacation and I didn't see her at school.
I didn't tell anyone, I was afraid to. I knew it was wrong
and dangerous and I was afraid that anyone who found
out about it would pull me out of it.

When school started up again I saw her at lunch.
You don't seem as friendly anymore, she said. She
would invite me over after school but I would make up
some excuse. I had to wait for him, go to him, that was
more important. After a while she began to understand
and stopped inviting me. Terecita had been hurt by so

many people that she didn't get angry at me for not wanting to be her friend anymore, didn't even question why. She just understood that sooner or later everyone got tired of her, used her up and abandoned her. She still smiled at me when she saw me. And then one day she came up to me, so shy, as though it was no longer her privilege, and she told me her mom was out of town on a business trip and did I want to come over and stay the night. And I said okay. I could walk to her house, it was that close to mine, and that afternoon after school we made cookies and watched movies and I tried, tried not to think of him. I told myself I was a normal high school girl having a normal after-school day with a friend doing normal things like watching videos and talking about relationships. We were sitting on her bed and she was telling me about boyfriends she had had, silly boyfriends like mine who just liked to kiss and hold hands, when I said, I'm seeing someone. Who? Terecita asked, as if it could be someone from school, something that simple. He's old, I said. He's not American. And I told her how we met, described it all in detail, told her what he looked like and how he sounded and what he did for a living, how every day I spent at his apartment. Then I told her about his wife and daughter, how they had gone to New York while she was having her next baby. Terecita just couldn't understand. But he's married, she said, he's married. What about his wife? Don't you feel sorry for his wife?

She didn't understand how you can't pick and choose, how someone having a wife and children isn't always enough to make you stop loving him. How sometimes even those things cannot take him away from you.

I tried not to think about his wife but I couldn't really feel sorry for her when I did. I felt sorry for her being herself, married to someone who loved someone else more. Too frightened and scared and anachronistic to leave him. He told me how happy it made her to do little things for him, to cook for him, clean up after him, bring him a glass of water, cut his meat for him. It was so easy for me to believe he loved her because of that only, even though he was always telling me what a wonderful human being she was.

No matter how hard I tried I could never be to him what she was. I could never wait on him hand and foot. I could do it for maybe a day at most. I couldn't show my love by giving him a back rub every single evening or getting up in the middle of the night to fix him a sandwich. It suited me, in a way, that I could never provide that kind of love for him. It explained things, explained why he would stay with her. So when he told me how intelligent she was, how sweet, how gentle, I somehow didn't believe it. He was saying it almost in defense, as if someone, maybe some part of him even, dared to deny it.

That awful week he went away to her, I would look down at my empty hands and wonder, Why didn't I do something for him when he was here? I could have washed the dishes, cleaned the apartment, cut his nails, ironed his shirts. I thought that if I had only done enough, worn myself out helping him and serving him, he would see how happy I could make him, he would stay with me. Always this feeling that if I could only do enough, he would notice and love me.

I knew he was going only because he called me from the airport. Said he was going, that his plane was leaving in fifteen minutes. He didn't even say goodbye. When I hung up the phone I went and sat down on my bed in my room. I wanted to go back to his apartment, to lie under the quilt on the couch, but he had taken the keys with him. Probably so that, when they came back together, she would not find me waiting for her there. Or equally bad, so that I couldn't come looking for him, unlock the door and find her there, in her apartment, innocently cooking dinner for her husband.

Once she came back to the apartment it would change. It would be a stranger's house, like when you walk down a strange street and see all the houses in a row, you can look in the windows, see the people moving around, watching TV maybe, you can imagine yourself being there, living with them, but you know you could never do anything so simple as open the door and step inside. That's how the place would change. It would change from a place where I was welcome, where I could sprawl out and take food from the fridge without asking and never feel uncomfortable, where, when I was alone, it became part of me, to just another closed door. If I came back, if I broke in when they weren't home, there would be new pictures on the walls, someone else's clothes, unfamiliar smells. I didn't want to know what it would be like.

Or maybe he didn't give me a key because he was afraid for his wife. Could he have thought I was capable of hurting her? It was something I thought about. If he left me a key I could sneak into the house when no one was home and put poison in her food or in her clothes, or wait until he was gone and shoot her point blank. But how could I do any of those things without killing him too? Murdering her with my own hands would be like death for him. Anything I did to her, even a scratch on her littlest toe, and he would never forgive me. What normal person could? After all, he loved her.

If I were to kill her it would be as revenge. Only after I understood how unhappy he had made me could I kill her and disappear somewhere, leave him to suffer in silence for the rest of his life. But if I wanted him back, if I was still in my right mind, I could never contemplate hurting her.

I believed I could poison her with thoughts, and the baby too. She would get sick in New York and die, and it wouldn't really be my fault. Or I could make her hate him and she would leave on her own. Would she? She would never leave him. She was the kind of woman who had never been alone, going straight from her parents' house to her husband's. She had never been lonely, had never been hurt, had never been rejected by a man since the only man she'd ever known was the one she was married to. She could never live without him.

I hated her so much, her ignorance, her trust were only more reasons why he stayed with her. Why he married her. She would always forgive him, always stand beside him even as he lied and cheated.

Nine

One night shortly before he left he was in a bad mood, he'd had a long day at work and he was tired of me, I had made a mess in the kitchen and forgotten to clean it up and had been watching cartoons when he came home. One of those days when he thought of me as a child who could never do anything right and although he didn't say anything, just went into the kitchen without speaking and put away the pans, loaded the dirty dishes into the dishwasher, I knew he was tired of me. We went to bed, but at three in the morning he still hadn't fallen asleep and neither had I. Both of us were anxious and upset because we felt that soon it would all be over, soon his child would be born. He missed her and didn't know what to do about me, and I was terrified of losing him. My love had never meant anything. I held him tightly, I was afraid of crying. Already the tears were pushing on the words, forcing them out. I love you, I said. You can't believe how much I love you. Maybe I do, he said. I told him I couldn't believe his wife loved him that way. That no one could love him as much as I did. You're everything to me, I said. My whole life is you. Everything I do, it's all in some way for you. No one can ever love you as much as I do. My wife does, he says. She says the same thing to me. That no one else can ever love me as much.

I imagined his wife lying with him in the same position, her head on his chest, listening to his heart, and I hated her for being so stupid. Never imagining that somewhere out there was a girl who loved him fiercely, who deserved him. Because although I never had any reason, any evidence, I knew that he loved me more. Hadn't he told me he would die without me? That he couldn't stay in this country without me? I questioned him along the lines of, You don't love me, do you? You don't care about me, do you? Hoping he would argue to the contrary. The very same way he set me up in sexual situations to test my loyalty. See my tears. Satisfied that I would go with someone else to please him but would hate it, all of it, because I didn't want anyone else. But this time, maybe because we were both so tired, he began to speak his mind. He had never really loved anyone in all his life. Never loved anyone so much he could give up everything to be with them, go crazy with love and die for them. It meant he had never loved me either. He couldn't. That was when I knew she would come back.

Ten

Jason was my first friend in high school and my first boyfriend ever. Although he wasn't much of a boyfriend. Other kids in my same grade were sexually active, one girl had Norplant, another couple had been going out since eighth grade. But I wasn't like everyone else. Some people might say I was sheltered. I never spent much time with kids my age. It was always just me and my mother, alone, wherever we went. I went to a different school almost every year, switching because there was always some reason why I didn't fit in. A teacher didn't like me, the kids were mean or stupid, the work was boring.

My mother was like that too, running away, rearranging what was not essential, changing the background of our lives as if that would change who we were. For a long time I thought it would, did.

I believed that she had to power to change me, buying me new clothes, sending me off to a new school. This time I would be the perfect child. No one here has seen the real me exposed. Like in first grade, keeping my head down on my desk. Almost all my early years in school were preoccupied with learning not to cry, learning to be tough and angry. I wanted to be strong. Even when everything was moving in a whirlwind around me I wanted to stand up straight and tall, a tree with roots firm, deep in the ground. That's why I was so stubborn.

I believed her words had the power to rewrite my past. It didn't matter what I thought about myself or thought I knew about myself, or what other people said. My mother always insisted she knew me best. Knew me doubly well, because she knew her child that was me since my very birth, and also knew the child that was her and what she became. She said, You're just like me.

Together we were like conspirators, deciding what our lives would be. My mother was the gay divorcee, alternately the heiress, I was the shining little rich kid. It didn't matter that we had no money. We deserved to have money and that made us the same as people who lived in fancy houses and bought two or three new cars with their six-figure salaries. We were better, even, because we had culture. We were educated, my mother with her BA from the state university and me with my honor-roll grades. I learned to look down on other people, even people who were successful. I resented them for their advantages, berated myself for not matching their achievements. There was always this constant competition and comparison. Why can't we be like everybody else? Or, why should we be like everybody else? Or, what if everybody else is better than us?

My friend Terecita was the only person I ever talked to who understood what it's like to have only one parent all to yourself. I don't think families with two or three kids and both parents can ever imagine the closeness, because with them, there are always extra people to act as buffers. To intercept the flow of love. You can maybe fall out of touch with your mother for a while because at some point you have more in common with your sister, your brother, your father. You can never allow one person to control you so completely, to master your thoughts, your memories, your dreams. My mother and I were like that, interlocked. Each of us was all the other had. Separate us and we would change, shrivel, die.

We told ourselves no one was ever good enough, intelligent enough, to include. No one would ever understand us the way we understood each other. I didn't think about any of this for the longest time and then I went away, found myself in another country about to get kicked out of my apartment because they said I didn't know how to live, and I was terrified. No one there loved me with that love. No one whose sole obligation was to me, mine to them. That was the first time I realized what family meant.

It changed when my mother married Don. I never thought it could. Maybe it was because I was growing up, now drawing knowledge and experience from books, teachers, places she could not imagine, could not dictate. Not because of the marriage. But there was someone else in the house now, and I felt a share of her love diverted, channeled away from me. I was so lonely and lost. That's what made it so easy.

Eleven

I don't know what I can say about your mother, he said when I told him. To raise a child like that on her own, well, that takes great strength. But she was very foolish, selfish. It isn't right to pull a child up from her roots.

That is when I really began to miss my grandmother. Here was someone who could devote all her days to loving just me. Her husband was dead, her children grown and married. Her life was spent looking after the house, bossing her sons, raising her grandchildren. I was her favorite, maybe because I was the oldest, maybe because I was the smartest. My grandmother felt that because my mother was American, a foreigner, she wasn't capable of raising me correctly; because my mother was an outsider, my grandmother felt all the more justified in luring me away from her. Because my mother barely understood Persian, she was powerless to interrupt the bond that developed between my grandmother and me. But although my grandmother was there always, and I mean in the sense that she was the most reliable presence in my life, the grownup I went to if I couldn't sleep at night, if I scraped my knee, if the other kids were teasing me, I didn't always understand her love for me. She was always screaming at me or chasing me around the house, always complaining that I was never quiet and that I pestered her all day long. Her two punishments, pinching and the silent treatment, were the ultimate torture and humiliation for me. At times, as when she went around the house deliberately ignoring the little person trailing after her but telling everyone she encountered how naughty her granddaughter had been that day, I thought she was just playing a joke, but I was also afraid that maybe she really hated me.

No one explained to me, I was too young, that we were leaving but I remember a few days before when everyone knew for certain that it was true, that the visas were approved and the plane reservations confirmed, I remember her being especially nice to me and how sometimes I would forget about her for a while, forget to look at her face because I was playing or making something busily, and when I did look at her there would be tears in her eyes. Why are you crying? I would ask and she would say, Come sit with me a while and pull me into her lap. Are you missing grandpa? I would ask, he had been dead since before I was born, and she would click her tongue No. I'm here, I'd say, and she'd say, That's true. And I never would have imagined the reason she was so sad was me. I remember her voice late at night yelling, always yelling when she spoke to the adults, to my parents espe-

cially, trying to bully them into staying. But my father
was her favorite and she was a little bit scared of him
so there wasn't much she could do.

Then we were gone. I don't remember the airport
scene, how everyone in the family came to see us off. I
don't remember my first impressions of America, how
it looked to me, child that had been born an expatriate.
I remember getting to know my father, because without the aunties and grandmother he was forced to
take more responsibility and spend more time with
me. I don't think he was very good with kids, because
when I was alone with him in the apartment he would
usually just turn on the TV for me and go into the
bedroom. I remember the cartoons of those years more
than anything. Smurfs, Scooby Doo, Bugs Bunny, Care
Bears in the Land of Care-A-Lot.

Maybe my father was the kind of man I would have
grown to know and appreciate only as an adolescent,
when he could begin to relate to me as an adult. Maybe
he would have been the salvation of my high school
years, the way they always say girls' fathers are closer
to them than their mothers at that time. He would have
shown me who I was, taught me to be proud of being
half Persian, of being an expatriate, of being different.
My father represented the truth to me, waiting to be
found, the truth about my past. My past through my

mother's eyes was like somebody's dream. Distorted, colored too brightly, too easily forgotten or misremembered.

Twelve

Of my second father, who only lasted a year and eight months, I remember just that one thing. I don't remember what he looked like, though we have pictures. Maybe the pictures displaced my memories of him. But everyone insists he was a bad person so of that I can be sure. I don't remember him being kind to me.

Sometimes I think that though I grew up without a father, I've been fathered by a lot of different men. My mother's three husbands, then Mekhti who was the first one I was able to choose for myself, if you can call it choosing.

I don't know if I chose him, if I did something to bring him into my life. Maybe I did something purposefully that other, normal girls, healthy ones, would not have done, like giving him my phone number or getting into his car late at night. Or maybe there was just some quality about me, some kind of openness, vulnerability that drew him to me. A sign that I was missing someone important from my life. Was it my fault? Was it something to do with the way I'd been raised? With my having so many different fathers? Being abandoned, divorced? Maybe it would have happened to any girl he decided he wanted. He always bragged to me what a marvelous talker he was, how he could persuade anyone of anything. Maybe I have no special susceptibility. I'll never know unless it happens again.

But it also seemed, a lot of times, that he wasn't in control either. At night he held me from behind, pushed his face into my shoulder, sighed deep sighs. He didn't know how to banish me from his life. Someone told me once, You filled a hole in his life he didn't know was there. Now, if you leave, he'll feel how empty it is.

So many nights we dragged each other down deep into depression, just sitting and talking about the direction we were going. He made such an effort to disguise his feelings for me, I think secretly he wanted me to ferret them out, to know. All I could feel was him, and when he left to go to work during the day, the whole apartment became a huge empty void, full of space nothing could fill. He worked as an assistant to some Russian mechanic, working at six dollars an hour until he had gained enough experience to work for an American repair shop that would pay a fair salary. He hated it (he hated all kinds of work) and he hated the way his hands always looked dirty. Not only was there black grease under his fingernails but it was even in the skin of his fingertips, tattooed right into the fingerprints. I loved his hands. I liked to hold two and three of his fingers at a time, feel them warm and living in my hand. I loved their smell, like salt, like blood, like car grease. I liked to press his hand to my lips, my cheek, forcing him to love me.

I'll never know how he felt about her coming back. I wish I could pry open his mind like a clock and look inside, turn gears here and there until the secret pops out. Yes or no. Love or no love. Like the fortune in a fortune cookie. I wish it were that simple.

Thirteen

Right after I began staying the night, that was our best time together. But then people began coming by, friends he had met here and there. Some of these people worked in the garage with him, some lived in the same building, some were people and friends of people that sold him weed. They started coming by, nice people at first, to sit and talk about nothing and drink a little, just get together in the evenings. Later they would take him out to restaurants, bars, whatever. At first I went too, but the atmosphere, the smoke and loud talk in other languages, made my stomach hurt. So he left me at home and stayed out all night. I would sit in the dark, I had turned off all the lights but the TV, and would sit there in the blue shadows, oblivious to the screen, wondering where he was and trying not to let myself get upset over someone not even mine. Because I never had any right to feel jealous or hurt or betrayed, as he said. Only his wife had that right.

Not allowing myself to feel anything I would sit and concentrate on the dark, on nothing until he came home, jumping every time I heard a knock on the walls or a key in somebody else's door. But when the people came it was worse.

Sometimes they would knock on the door at eleven, twelve o'clock. I would be sleeping and he would be out in the living room, watching TV as if waiting for them. They were so loud they woke me up. And once I came out, they wouldn't let me back in. They teased me, the men from his job and the addicts and the dealers, the women who lived off their boyfriends' paychecks, for being young and tender, easily offended. There were girls my age who sat on his lap and laughed at everything he said. Young men, college age, who worked as waiters and store clerks and sold pot on the side to make extra money. None were American. The older people, people his age, had been here just two or three years at most so they spoke only Russian or Persian or Armenian. The young people had mostly grown up here and spoke every language including English but used so much slang it made my head ache.

The women I hated especially. The young girls so thin in their tight black skirts and brown lipstick who giggled at me, the older women, still beautiful, who got falling down drunk and ran their hands over him. All of them looking at me like I was keeping them from having fun. The men were nicer. They talked to me, flirted with me, and in the beginning the attention flattered me. Never had so many men looked at me in that way. But after I realized what they were after, I silently hated them. The older men who looked even older than they really were, the young men who came in jeans and t-shirts and whose voices were always stoned. They sat and smoked, and talked and smoked, and drank and talked the way Eastern people can for hours. Sitting on the floor at his feet, just breathing in, I became stoned for the first time. I tried to say something and stopped and then started again because it seemed like the words were tripping over themselves, coming out either too fast or too slow, and then because it all seemed too funny I just gave up and laughed, and the others who were all listening intently to me laughed too, and someone said, She's stoned.

Once the glamour wore off, there were only one or two of them I really liked. There was Albert, who lived on the first floor, apartment A-102. He had graduated from a chemical engineering institute in Armenia when he was young and he liked to talk to me. I showed him my chemistry textbook, the chapter we were on this month, Chapter 8, the Periodic Table of Elements. Mekhti would just wave his hand, tell about how he threw a chair at the principal and was carried out of school three times by the police for rough behavior. I never learned anything in school, he said. I quit school as soon as I was old enough to start making money. But Albert sat beside me patiently while I explained about the tests I had taken and what grades I had gotten.

When I stopped going to school he was the only one who noticed. He noticed that my test scores were getting lower and lower and asked, How much did you study? My answer would be, A week, then, Three days, then, The night before, then, An hour before class.

When they had all gone home at three or four in the morning we would go into the bedroom to get ready for bed and Mekhti would question me. Who did you like? What did you think of Abram? He's a handsome man. What about Yulia? Have you ever wanted to make love to a girl? And he would go on and on, not just aroused but excited, trying to tempt me, trip me up. I noticed you talking to Albert, he would say time and again. You like him, don't you? I would shrug my shoulders. Do you think he's attractive? I would shrug again. Albert was okay, in a fatherly kind of way. He had a nice nose, was tall and had wavy black hair. The next question, Would you sleep with him? Mekhti told me that sex was the best experience life had to offer and that a young person like me should never pass up an opportunity to experience everything. That if I just relaxed and stopped feeling guilty I would enjoy it. I thought there was something wrong with me. I thought Albert would be gentle. He could make me relax, maybe it was true. Do you want to sleep with him, Mekhti asked. I could arrange it in six seconds. But I would never agree like that. Especially not with Albert,

who was my friend. I was intelligent enough to know
not to ruin a friendship with such a nice person.

Night after night, after they had gone home, he pressured me. He wanted to see me with a woman, with
other men. That was the only thing that could excite
him anymore. He said I would like it. He described it
for me. I told him I would do anything for him, but I
wouldn't enjoy it. I knew that about myself if nothing
else.

I was gradually feeling myself disappear, feeling
the old person leave, the person who had opinions,
values all her own. Mekhti was taking her place, train-
ing what was left of me to be someone like him. Inside
I felt collapsed. I didn't know right or wrong anymore.
Whatever he told me I should try, I did. All of it hurt,
all of it made me grind my teeth in anger and humiliation and pain. I cried to him. I screamed, I want you,
only you. But he said that was not enough. Sometimes
I almost convinced myself it was fun. It helped to be
drunk and stoned at the same time. Then it didn't
really matter. I couldn't feel my own body, it was like it
wasn't happening to me. The strange thing is during
those times, if I thought about myself at all, pictured
myself, I saw a different girl. She was just a body, a
featureless face with my name on her. I walked through
a school like a zombie, tired and stoned from the night

before that was actually a week, a month of nights with no sleep, and was avoided by everyone. At school I listened to the lectures on chemistry, geometry, American history that once seemed to me the most important part of the day. Now I sat and my mind wandered to the night before, how I had been woken up out of sleep, how there had been smoke and laughter and somewhere, I knew, eyes watching. I felt like everyone around me must be able to tell. In PE I was afraid of my body. I thought there must be some visible signs.

When he left for New York it was different. The parties, which had been going on for weeks to kill his worries, were over. None of them knew where I lived, where I had gone. I don't think they cared. I stayed at home now, or rather I slept there and found various places to put myself all day. Home was too innocent an environment. I went to school every day because I couldn't bear to be alone with my thoughts. For the first time I thought I might do something dangerous. Scratch or cut myself or swallow pins. Someone told me about people escaping Soviet prisons that way, by swallowing a special cross made of pins until the cramps and bleeding necessitated their removal to a hospital.

Before, it had been impossible to tell anyone. I had been too ashamed, too afraid someone might take me away from him, afraid that just talking about it would cause it to fall apart. But now that it was over, nothing mattered anymore. When the English teacher stopped me after class and remarked on my perfect attendance for that week and asked, Are things going better for you? I answered no before I could stop myself. She said, I'll still be here after seventh period.

I didn't want to tell her or anyone on the surface but underneath I must have wanted very badly to unburden my conscience because it was like my feet had a mind of their own, as soon as seventh period was over they headed in the direction of the English room. The English teacher seemed genuinely surprised, too, to find me there. Come in, she said, and I sat down, and she said some things and I said some things, the kind of things you say to get a difficult conversation going, and then suddenly I broke down and told her everything. How we met, how we lived, why I was out of my mind and hopeless with fear and despair. I just know I'm going to die if she comes back, I told her through tears. I won't be able to live, knowing she's there. I love him so much, I love him so much. It seemed vitally important that she understand.

She listened quietly and never once showed that she was shocked or disgusted or angry. And then, when I had told it all she leaned forward, put her hand on my shoulder and said, Do you know what statutory rape

is? She waited for me to produce a yes. Then she said,
What he has done to you is a criminal offense and he
can be arrested, put in jail, even deported for it. As he
should be. All you have to do is tell me his name.

I choked. Say it! I couldn't say it. I can't tell you, I
said. He isn't a criminal. I'm sorry. I jumped up, knocking over a desk as I ran away.

Fourteen

A lot of people were kind to me and tried to help me but I just couldn't accept it. Pure good intentions scared me and time and again I ran away. I couldn't even say thank you. There was Terecita, who tried to be my friend, and Jason, who wanted me to love him, and Albert who lived downstairs and always tried to clean up the mess Mekhti made of me. My English teacher, who expected so much of me, my other teachers. They gave me so many chances, so many it was impossible for me to make blunders out of all of them.

It was the last month of the first semester that my grades began to slip. Because after I met Mekhti I didn't have the heart to study. All vacation, on those wet December mornings, I took long walks to the lake and back, ate nothing but milk and toast, and waited by the phone. My stomach was upset all the time, my hands trembled. My parents wanted to know why I was so jumpy. When school started I was distracted. I could study but not for very long. I got only B's on some of my finals at the end of January, but that wasn't enough to alter my perfect report card for the semester. Afterward was when things really began to go downhill. Some of my teachers, the ones my English teacher had been able to convince that I was going through a difficult time at home, no details added, gave me A's even though I missed tests and didn't turn in half my homework. The rest gave me D's and F's. My English teacher somehow thought she saw a spark in me, something magical and whole, and whenever she caught me off guard, alone, she hinted that my future was something grand but far away from here. She told me, If you just get through these difficult times, if you can get away to school in a few years, it will be your salvation. You can make it, I know you can.

Sleeping in Mekhti's apartment, dozing off to the sound of talking and a woman's loud, drunken laugh, I had certain dreams. I dreamed that some part of my body, a scratch or a scab, split open and peeled off and when I looked inside my arm or leg it was hollow. I could even see the light shining through my skin from outside like it was plastic. Or, an interesting twist, my navel would grow bigger and bigger until my belly was a huge gaping hole. When I would wake up with this dream in the morning, after Mekhti had gone to work, I would sit in bed and hold myself under the covers, and I could not go to school. The whole day was spent in bed or in the living room watching TV, walking around the apartment, hands on arms, touching myself to make sure I was all really there.

Fifteen

In April it was decided that I take the college entrance
exams. I didn't understand why but my teacher said,
Just wait and see. My eyes were red all the time and
school was just a headachy blur to me, I thought the
idea of me taking a test must be some kind of joke. But
there was a part of me that wanted out of this life, that
would do anything to escape, and that part managed to
pull me away from Mekhti temporarily. I came home
for a few nights, slept well, rested. The house was so
quiet at night, unlike Mekhti's apartment with its laughter, voices, smoke. The silence was scary. I hadn't slept
for nights on end but, lying alone in a bed too big for
me, in a shadowy room of blue and white, I couldn't
close my eyes. I was afraid of where I would go if I did
sleep. The house and the silence would swallow me up.
I walked downstairs at night into the cold kitchen,
switched on the light, ate a piece of cheese. I wanted to
call him but couldn't let myself. Once, when I did call,
a woman's voice answered the phone over a roar of
voices and laughter. Another time, it was just his voice,
sleepy, Allo? Both times I hung up.

Leaving had been easy. I said simply that I had a big
assignment coming up in school and needed time to

prepare. He had driven me home. I didn't tell him about the test. I was afraid somehow he would be angry, resentful. He would think that I was trying to escape him by wanting to go to college, that I was trying to escape into my old life, my interest in school.

On the day of the test I had to be at school earlier than usual. The test began at seven. I brought four new pencils and an eraser with me and sat down in a seat assigned by alphabetical order. A teacher read us the instructions and we began, fifty minutes per section. It was difficult to concentrate. I would wander off, remembering. But each time I forced myself back, forced myself to think only of the questions, one at a time. Math was easiest to focus on, reading comprehension the hardest. At one point I almost gave up and filled in all the circles at random, the way I did usually. I didn't want to be here, I didn't want to prepare for my future, I didn't have enough energy to worry about myself. But four hours later when it was finally over I had answered every question. I had cheated a little, gone back to the verbal comprehension section when I had a little time left over after analogies and antonyms, but I was glad. And when the results came back six weeks later, about the same time as my report card with three A's, one D and two F's, my English teacher was ecstatic. I knew you could do it, she said.

I hadn't thought about the test after I'd taken it. I hadn't had time to, except during the week Mekhti was in New York. Then I began hoping I would do well, so that I could get far away from him. It seemed to be my only avenue of escape. I wanted to be applauded again, to be the center of hopes and expectations again. I felt like that person had been killed inside me. When I thought back to her, how she had triumphed over grades and math tests and oral reports, she seemed very silly to me, very childish. How could I care about those things now when there were days I felt like the marrow was being sucked out of me, everything special in my life broken into bits and blown away? Those things I used to love and care about just seemed so dark and small. How could I go back to being that girl who believed she knew everything, could do everything? Her skin was too small for me now and I no longer knew how to be her.

My English teacher came to me with an application for junior college. She wanted me to apply and forget about coming back to high school that fall. I marked all the boxes, filled in all the blanks, and signed it and gave it back. It seemed like a betrayal to tell Mekhti, not to tell him. Later, when he left for New York and it looked like everything was over, I was glad I had done it. Now I would have somewhere to go.

Sixteen

Sooner or later alone in his apartment I noticed her clothes in his closet. I never went so far as to try them on; in all honesty I was afraid even to touch them. She was smaller than I was. She liked foreign people's clothes, things no one else wears, leopard print blouses, short black skirts, mohair berets in navy and maroon. She had a real fox stole, the kind with the fox head and paws still attached, ragged holes where the eyes would be. Mekhti was very proud of his wife's stole and told me of all the Americans who had complimented her on it but it always made me a little sick to think of that poor little beast dying just for her. I took it out sometimes and laid it across my knees, petted it like it was hurt but alive, and imagined it running through Russian forests, its silver fur streaking through the trees. Of course, it never ran free in its life. Surely it was raised on some Soviet fur farm, lived out its life in a cramped wire cage and died by an electric shock that was guaranteed not to spoil the fur. I hated her as if she had killed it.

She had a box of jewelry too, gold chains and necklaces, rings with red and pink stones, earrings. Most of it was from Samarkand and the gold was a strange pinkish color. Each piece had a special stamp on the underside, the personal stamp of the goldsmith. He bought her some jewelry after they came here, too. Rhinestone pins shaped like butterflies and turtles, a gold-plated watch from Kmart. I came to the conclusion that they had flashier tastes than Americans, that everything about them, every shoe, scarf, earring had to wink and glitter and turn heads. To me it all looked cheap and childish.

The day I found the box of jewelry was the day Mekhti came home early from work in a happy mood. He took everything out of the box and proudly explained the history of each piece. How the gold watch had been for her birthday, the necklace for their anniversary, the gold ring for a time in Samarkand when he hadn't been a very good husband, the butterfly pin from Kmart just because he loved her. He had never bought me anything except candy. Not even anything fancy in a box but just some chocolate shapes like Santa Claus faces wrapped in colored foil. Why should he give me anything? I had no right to anything from him. He always told me I had no right to compete with his wife, no right to jealousy. Maybe I was just stupid but I could never understand why nothing more than an official document and a ceremony gave her more right to him than I had. Was she a better person? Had she suffered more? Did she need love more than I did?

When I talked it over with Terecita she said, Don't you feel ashamed? Ashamed of what, I asked. You're taking him away from his wife, she said, his family. But it seemed like I needed him much more. I could not imagine anyone feeling about him the way I did. No one could love him as much, need him that way, worship him with every last drop of her soul. He had been with his wife for eleven years. She was used to him, depended on him. But my need was fresh and raw.

One day I asked him, couldn't he box up his wife's clothes and things so I wouldn't have to be reminded, every day, that it was her apartment, that I was just passing through? We got into a mild fight over that. He said, I never gave you any hope. You knew all along she would come back. I don't want to put away her things, I need to remember her. Boxing up her clothes as if she had died would be dangerous since already her health was so precarious, he still loved her and thought of her every day and he said, kindly, I never gave you any excuse to believe that I would leave my wife.

No matter what happened to me, no matter what kind of experience I had, I still had this idea that no matter how many people you said you loved, there was always one you loved most. And when he told me, I love you both in different ways, I was never satisfied. Most of the time I resigned myself to believing he loved her best. He said to me, I've known you four months, her eleven years. Which love do you think is strongest? But sometimes I wondered if it wasn't me he loved best. At times I didn't know whether that would be better or worse for me. Could I survive on the knowledge that he wanted to be with me but was tied by tradition, by family loyalty, to her?

Seventeen

Terecita had a special way of sitting, one leg crossed over her knee and the front of that leg hooked under the calf of the other, her body bent over her desk, her hair making a tent around her face and shoulders like she wanted to hide them from the rest of us. She always wore brown Mary Janes with white socks and her bare legs looked so smooth and brown. The times I stayed over at her house, we slept in the same bed, and sometimes during the night her arm or leg would brush against mine, giving me a strange shivery feeling. It was like my own skin touching me. Her house was small, rented and always cold. The cement floor in her room was uncarpeted. Like me, Terecita didn't live too far from school, and she whined about having to walk home. Once or twice I walked home with her, the days I went to her house to make long distance calls. Just before her house you had to go through these woods where there was just a dirt path, the kind of place that would be fun to play in as a kid. The path was steep and you had to skid down it. Terecita went first and I came behind her. I envied her long long legs, also her dark straight hair and huge black eyes. Like her father's, no doubt. Terecita took it for granted that she had her father in her. She had seen him so many times, she knew what he looked like, knew how she resembled him. She could imitate the way he spoke English, the expressions he used. I couldn't even remember the sound of my father's voice. Once I dreamed about him but whenever he opened his mouth to speak there was nothing, silence, the words coming to me like telepathy. I feel sorry for you, Terecita would say. We felt sorry for each other, and secretly each felt glad to be superior, which was why we were friends.

You shouldn't be so interested in your dad, Terecita said. I mean, I understand why you want to find him and all that, but you'll probably just be disappointed if you do. He probably isn't any better than my dad.

Terecita's dad was remarried. The wife was only a few years older than us and since she couldn't decide whether it was more appropriate to be mother or sister to Terecita she just ignored her. There were also two spoiled little half sisters who ate only noodles. If I were you, Terecita said, I would just forget about finding him.

But I couldn't forget, because deep in my heart I knew my father was nothing like Terecita's. We were different, like my mother always said, superior. My father would not have remarried. When I pictured him, I always imagined him in business. He would be the

president or CEO of a large company and he would
work out of an office of chrome and glass with a large
picture window. He would have a private secretary
who would announce me, Your daughter is on the
phone. All I knew about him was his master's in business from UCLA, where he met my mother.

At Mekhti's apartment, lying on the bed, I would
compare his hands to mine. Our hands had exactly the
same shape, same curve. It didn't matter whether they
were laid flat side by side or palm to palm or if they
were clutching something like a cup or a pencil. Even
our fingernails were the same, not square like some
people's or ending too soon of our fingertips, but perfect. Perfect ovals. And we both had the same mark, a
freckle on the palms of our left hands, on the fleshy part
below the thumb. The mark, he said, meant that I was a
queen among women and he was a king among men. It
was extremely important to me that we have the same
hands. I thought of them as brother and sister hands,
father and daughter hands.

Eighteen

For a long time I held the list in front of me and stared at it, stared at the phone, stared at the list again. Terecita was standing over my shoulder, she really wanted me to call. Come on, she said, you haven't tried any of them yet. One of these could be the one. But I didn't want to do it. I liked that piece of paper the way it was, all the names, all fourteen, penciled in a vertical row so carefully. After the operator had given them to us, I recopied them neatly. I didn't want to see them crossed off, scratched out. I liked to leave things whole.

Fear made me seize up during the rings, before he answered. A man's voice said, Allo? There was an accent. Would he still have an accent, after all these years? Hi, I said. I explained who I was. I'm not your father, he said. But maybe we're related. He was a student, he said, a graduate student at UCLA. Twenty-eight, dark hair, dark eyes. Terecita was listening at my ear. I like to go clubbing, he said. He asked me questions. How old I was, what color my eyes were, how much did I weigh. I would really like to meet you, he said. Do you have family that you visit in LA?

When I hung up I was really excited. Maybe this is a

start, I said. Maybe he knows my family. Maybe he knows someone who knows my father. We could take the bus down to LA. Terecita said, He just wants to sleep with you. Middle Eastern guys can be like that. We didn't make any more calls after that and although I kept the list, I put it away somewhere where I wouldn't have to look at it.

Nineteen

My parents thought that I was living at Terecita's when all the time I was with Mekhti. I told them her mom was away on one business trip, then another, that Terecita didn't like staying alone at night. I who had always been so proud of my truthfulness became very accomplished at lying. Last year, I told them, Terecita's house had been broken into and things stolen while everyone was sleeping. The police never caught the people who did it and every since then Terecita had been terrified to sleep in the house alone because she was afraid they would come back. When the business trip excuse wore thin I told them that Terecita's mother had been transferred to another state but that Terecita had agreed to stay until the end of the school year before moving too, seeing as how I could stay in the house with her. Otherwise she would have to move and start a new school in the middle of the semester. That excuse was partly true because her mom really had been offered another job in Nevada for the same company, only she was still making up her mind whether or not to accept it.

Whenever I stayed the night at Terecita's, her mom would drive us to the Japanese grocery downtown where we would buy strange snacks, shrimp and sweet potato chips, crackers that came with strawberry frosting for dipping. That would be our dinner, and we would eat it watching TV on the living room floor. There are certain houses where you only sit on the furniture and others where the most comfortable place is the floor. At Don's house, floors were for walking and standing on and the chairs and couches were for sitting, but at Terecita's house there was only one couch and that was reserved for her mom who was tired from working all day.

Terecita had a piano, an antique upright that even had brass candlestick holders. Her grandma had paid for her to have lessons in the third grade and she magnanimously taught me what she remembered of "Send In The Clowns" and "The Winds of War." Mekhti had an electronic keyboard in his apartment on loan from a friend. When he was gone to work I would switch it on and plink at the keys. There were three demo songs recorded that you could play with the press of a button, and I went through all of those first. Then I would go through all one hundred and twenty voices just to hear the sound of them and all the sixty rhythms from Country Western to Calypso. By then I usually got tired and switched it off. But Mekhti could play very well. As a teenager he had played in a band that performed at weddings in the mountain villages for Tadjiks and Uzbeks as well as for modern families in the cities. He told me how it was customary for everybody at the wedding to shower the musicians with money, thousands of dollars in a single night. When his friends came over to drink he would play, and sometimes in the morning before he left for work, I would wake up to hear him playing alone in the next room and sometimes singing. Albert told me that he could play the guitar just as well, but since there was no guitar I never got the chance to hear him. Everyone, all of his friends, talked about how well Mekhti played the guitar and all the Russian songs he knew. It was something he had learned while in the army.

Whenever I stayed over at Terecita's house I had trouble sleeping. She was one of those people who have to fall asleep listening to the radio and it would keep me awake, listening to the lyrics. Then during the night it was always too warm, sleeping with another body, or too cold, because Terecita would pull all the covers over to her side. And I was the kind of sleeper used to sprawling about. At night I would forget and as soon as my skin brushed against hers I would wake up. Shrink into a ball and try to be as still as possible so she would not wake up. I felt as ashamed as if I'd tried to kiss her.

In the morning I was always the first to wake up. It

had always been this way no matter whose house I
was spending the night at. Even if we had stayed up
until two or three the night before, I invariably woke
up at first light. The only thing to do then was read, so
I pulled out Terecita's mother's Latino-American novels from the bookcase next to the bed and read as
quietly as possible until Terecita woke up too. What
seems strange to me now is all the times I slept at
Mekhti's apartment, I always woke up late, well into
morning. On weekdays he either had to shake me
awake or just leave me there, so that the apartment was
empty when I woke up. He reset the alarm before he
left so that I could get up in time for school but even
so I never made it. I would hear it go off in my sleep
and my arm would reach up on its own and my hand
would hit the off button. My brain never even woke up.
On weekends he wouldn't bother to wake me up at
all, just slip out quietly to prepare breakfast. Bread with
cheese spread and pate or scrambled eggs with tomato.
And by the time I staggered out of the bedroom sleepy-
eyed at ten, eleven or twelve o'clock, the breakfast
would be cold crumbs and he would be sitting on the
couch watching TV. I would come to him, sit on his lap,
and he would smooth my wild hair, asking, How did
you sleep? That was how he always greeted me in the
beginning, when we first met. After he stepped out of
his car, instead of, Hello, how are you, he would say,
How did you sleep last night?

Mornings at Terecita's house we made pancakes out
of muffin mix, and neither of us was sure how much
batter to pour into the pan or how long to cook it, so
what we ended up with was gobs of bubbly dough or
scorched leathery little rounds. We generally made too
much. It was the only thing I ever saw Terecita eat a lot
of. Usually she and her mom made only salads or
tortillas with melted cheddar cheese. Once their dinner was a bag of potato chips. I could never eat and be
full at their house. I would find myself daydreaming
of something, of tart green apples or baked potatoes
with sour cream and bacon bits or a turkey sandwich
or a hamburger, and nothing else could satisfy me.
And the way they bought their groceries, they bought
just one sack at a time, enough to last for a few days
only. We always bought carloads, much too much for
just two people, and our refrigerator was packed so
full that the things in the back began to rot before
anyone found them. Mekhti's refrigerator wasn't like
anybody else's, it was packed full of meat. Thick juicy
steaks, boneless chicken breasts, beef ribs. I don't
know what it looked like when his wife lived there. He
didn't know how to make anything except shish kebab,
so breakfast and lunch was takeout or McDonald's, and
then after work sometimes he would spend two or
three hours marinating and grilling dinner for himself.
I never ate any, just smelling it cooking for so long

made me sick.

But whenever I opened Terecita's refrigerator there was nothing but a half-gallon carton of milk, salad dressing, and lettuce. There was nothing in their cupboards except for cereal and pancake mix. I was always afraid to take food without asking because I never knew what they were saving for dinner that night. If I made a sandwich out of that last piece of chicken or poured myself that last cup of milk, they might have to go back to the store or eat plain potato chips. I never understood that way of living until I was on my own and I kept my own refrigerator empty, buying just a few things at a time because I kept thinking that any day I would take the next flight home. I wanted to leave everything behind me empty.

Twenty

Terecita had a lot of new clothes. Once she took me with her to the mall to buy a pair of new jeans, and she spent hours parading in front of mirrors, trying on and discarding. I always knew that one reason she was my friend was that next to me she felt beautiful.

It was always a mystery to me how if Terecita and her mother were really so poor, Terecita was always getting money here and there to buy new clothes. I had almost no new clothes. My mother was always begging to let her buy me some new outfits, but I refused. There was nothing I hated more than being dragged into expensive stores and having to watch myself in the mirror trying on clothes that weren't me, feeling like a circus poodle or a bear in a tutu. Whenever there was some occasion, a funeral or a fancy dinner, I borrowed my mother's clothes. Everything smelled like her no matter how much she wore it or didn't wear it. Her smell was the smell of fine department stores, of face cream, perfume, lipstick that sometimes smeared onto the necks of her sweaters. You're lucky that you have my long neck, my mother would say when I was still five, six years old and shaped like a tree stump. She was always seeing herself in me where I couldn't and making pronouncements as though, by saying them, she could make them true. Transform me, a shapeless, ugly little girl into someone beautiful and gifted, radiant with her love. She talked about me like I was raw material, a jewel in the rough. You're going to be tall, she said. You can be a model when you grow up. You're lucky you're not insecure like other kids, she'd say. That's because you always knew you had a mother who loved you. She seemed to see my future self inside me so clearly that it came as a real shock to me when I realized I had grown into someone very different and would never be all the things she said I would. All along I had never doubted her power.

Twenty-one

Not long after my parents divorced, my mother's parents sold their house and moved to a condo and gave her some of the money, like an inheritance, they said. Not enough to put us in the lap of luxury, but enough to take away most of our financial worries for a while. My mother worked on and off throughout my childhood, between marriages. As a saleswoman in an expensive department store, an office secretary, a clerk in a grocery store, a telephone receptionist. Every time we moved, she changed jobs. Whenever she began to get tired of her job, and I started complaining about school, we started looking for a new place to begin a new life. The department store job was probably her favorite. She loved showing off the store like it was her own. Though I imagine it must have been hard for her to spend her days at the beck and call of rich but ungifted women, picking out silks to bring out the color of their eyes and jewelry to accent their vacation tans, all the while thinking how much prettier she was than Mrs. So-and-So and how Mrs. Such-and-Such for all her husband's money had never even completed college. It was so easy to imagine what she was thinking because I knew her so well. But there was always something more, something that made my thoughts of her seem too childish, too simple. I knew what she was like on the surface, knew her gestures, her words, but underneath all of that everything was riotous, a swirling center I could not penetrate. My mother knew all of me. Up until Mekhti anyway. All my likes and dislikes, fears and inhibitions, experiences the way you can flip open a well-worn book to any page and begin reading. I was like that for her. A page you could read front and back, nothing hidden in between. But although I exposed my all to her, she never explained herself to me. And there were parts of her, parts from before I was born and from things that happened when I wasn't there or wasn't around or could not see, that I would never know about her. The thought that my mother, the person I loved most and had studied more than anyone else in the world, had been several completely different people without me, was unsettling. I couldn't imagine her without me, couldn't imagine a time when I was not the driving force of her life and the center of her existence.

I loved to come see her in her department store job after school. I loved to play hide and seek inside the racks of clothes and feel their bright colors brush against my cheeks and fingers. I also loved to wander into the makeup department and play with all the perfume bottles. Some were shaped like diamonds, others like donuts, one like an exquisite pink ballerina. I begged my mother to buy one for me and when she finally did, I scandalized her by pouring all the expensive contents down the drain. It was only the bottle I wanted.

One place we lived, we kept a horse. That is, we rented one at a private stable and two or three times a week my mother drove me out to ride it and take lessons. My grandparents thought it was a terrible extravagance and a total waste of (their) money but my mother had just gotten the divorce from Glen and she felt she had to do something to cheer me up. She bought me a little English riding outfit with a riding hat and everything. But the next time we moved, which was in the middle of my third grade year, the horse stayed behind.

Twenty-two

I couldn't always call him my father. Especially during my mother's second marriage, he was her first husband, my first father (not my father) or just his name. It seemed impolite, a kind of disrespect to talk about him as my father in front of Glen or Don or my mother's male friends. We tried not to talk about him at all. When my mother was angry with him, still carrying a grudge, which was all the time, she called him by his name, Ali. She would spit his name out like something bitter she'd bitten into by mistake. Sometimes, though, when she was in a light mood she would reminisce about him and then she would call him Your Father. And that always seemed unnatural to me, as though it was it was a lie. I didn't have a father. I didn't like the way she said it, it was as if linking me to him—Your Father—was pushing me from her.

I envied other girls who could call all the people in their lives by a relationship, a special name. They could talk about their mother, their father, their sister, their boyfriend. Whenever I used the word father I always had to explain myself. That word, father, was an empty space no one could fill. And yet there was his name, Ali. It was easier, especially when talking to people who knew my mother, to call him that. Ali, my Persian father. Mekhti was the other person in my life who was that way. There was no relationship word that could explain him. There was Terecita my friend, Jason my boyfriend, there was my mother, and then there was Mekhti, whose name left all possibilities open.

At one point he started saying he thought it was still possible for us all to be happy together. He could introduce me to his wife as a volunteer from the language school. I could come over to visit on evenings and weekends, when his wife would be home, and we could talk together in the living room while she was in the kitchen cooking or even sitting there beside us. He couldn't see me as often as now, but the important thing was that he would still see me. We could still be best friends, and it wouldn't be a secret any longer. I could tell my parents, he could tell his wife and family. We can lose everything else, he said, all I want is to be able to see you from time to time, talk to you. At the very least we still have to be friends. His eyes hungry, his eyes would always speak to me even if nothing else were left of him. What he proposed, my coming back to that apartment every day but as his guest and exchanging pleasantries with his wife as we sat and visited together, was so bizarre, but wasn't it what I wanted? Just to be friends, and never to have to feel his hot hands, breath? But when he began to talk like

this it was always me who capitulated, who could not
compromise. I who would crawl up from behind and
put my arms around his neck, kiss his cheek and ear so
that we'd agree our relationship could never be only
platonic. I can't be next to you and not touch you, I
would say. And it was true. I could not talk to him
without physically touching him some way. We would
be standing talking and I would unconsciously step
toward him, slip my hands inside his jacket. It was
like we weren't close enough, couldn't hear each other
speak unless we were touching. Sometimes he would
say, All right, from now on I'm going to try not to
touch you. And I would spoil it by taking his hand or
touching his leg.

But the way I touched him was different. I just wanted
to get close and that was enough. To hold onto his
hand or stroke his skin like a charm, keep touching
and I won't disappear. I didn't want to arouse him. I
had no sexual thoughts although he obviously didn't
understand how I could hug or kiss and not feel that
way. For me, the touching stopped there. But I would
touch him and his breathing would get loud and heavy
and he would run his hands all over me roughly and
begin to take off my clothes, for him every touch went
that way. It was a small, stupid thing I always forgot
and then, later, when it would start all over again, I
could only grind my teeth and endure it. After all, I had

brought it upon myself. You torture me, he said. How do you expect any man to endure it? And my answer always was, But that wasn't what I had in mind. Touch for him and touch for me, it shows how differently we perceived each other.

He said, You could even come live with us. He saw my shocked expression and said, What can my wife do about it? A young girl, trouble at home, no place to go. Of course we would take you in.

He wanted so badly to contain our relationship and control it as if it could ever be as simple, as one-dimensional, as just friends or boyfriend-girlfriend. It was like a cancer that grew and grew, invading every other part of our lives and squeezing until nothing else was left. Simple relationships, like friend or boyfriend, are easy, you can replace them. But who could we ever find to reach into as many places in each other's lives?

Twenty-three

Jason wasn't my boyfriend the way I felt about it, but
he was the first friend I made in high school. I think
we made better friends than a couple. He was nerdy
like me, with curly blond hair and glasses, and he read
Ayn Rand and made cynical jokes with the teachers.
Both of us could appear very confident if you questioned us about books, science, politics, but with anything personal, with each other, we were shy, afraid of
doing something wrong and spoiling it. We talked
about sex of course, about whether people our age
should do it and about how horny we were, but together we didn't do much more than hold hands. We
weren't interested in anything else yet. Once or twice,
while watching a steamy movie on TV, we felt com-
pelled to grab each other, but it was more out of curios-
ity and a feeling that, if everyone else is doing it, we
should too, rather than any real passion. I could never
think of Jason as a guy. He had thick glasses that would
have gotten in the way, a big nose and a soft belly. I'm
sure I excited him just about as much as he did me. He
was so surprised when I began to talk about it, really
talk about it. It was an unspoken agreement between
us that we would joke about it all we wanted, but
neither of us wanted to do it and we never would, not

with each other, not in high school. Jason still dreamed
he would wait until he was married. What are you two
waiting for? Mekhti said. Here you say you have a
boyfriend, but you aren't even sleeping with him. He
said Jason must not be normal if he didn't ask for it.
That I must not be normal either, not to want it. That I
just didn't know what I was missing. Try it with him, he
said. And I did, but it wasn't easy. I made up my mind
I wanted it over. I wanted at least to know what it was
like, so I would know what people meant when they
talked about it and so people like Mekhti would stop
harassing me. I had an angry vengeance, I would do it
or else. Jason thought, rightly, that I didn't know what
I wanted, what I was doing. He asked, Are you sure you
want to go through with this? Yes, I said, through my
teeth. I was going to get it over with or die trying. It was
morning in his parents' house on a teacher conference
day. We had no school and his parents were at work.
This is the day I want to do it, I said.

Before that I had made several failed attempts to
seduce him, so that passion would carry him away and
do the rest for me. One day when we were watching TV
on the couch I tried unzipping his pants but he pulled
away from me. What are you doing, he asked, looking
at me like I had suddenly gone crazy.

As soon as we started it, I knew I didn't like Jason,

had stopped liking him, and would never be able to like him again. I remember we had a vague idea that the girl had to be ready first but we weren't sure what to do and then it wouldn't go in and we tried to force it. It was very painful. I was sore for two days afterward and when I went to pee there was this pink smear on the toilet paper. Jason told me it had hurt for him, too. He showed me where his foreskin had ripped. Afterward we went for a walk. It still hurt like hell and I remember being so full of fury, like there was a clawing animal inside me and the violence of our experience that morning had only now woken it up. I feel like running, I said. We raced to the end of the block but I didn't stop running until I was red in the face and there was no air inside me, my insides a flaming furnace. Jason caught up with me, wheezing. It's like you were running away from me, he said. I was still too furious to answer.

He was hurt when I didn't talk to him the next day. At first he thought I was angry because of what we'd done. It's okay, he said, I love you. We can get married. I didn't mean for it to happen this way. But before long he understood that I had used him. Slut, he called me. Tramp. Is that all you want from other people? I couldn't let myself feel sorry for him so I just made fun of him to myself. A guy whining that he'd had his virginity stolen.

It was like those scary rumors you hear, stories, actually, where the teenage kid who wants to join a gang has to steal something, commit a crime, and he kills a lady and cuts out her heart or cuts her head off and brings it to the gang leader. Only what I stole was not something tangible or even something you could name. I stole from other people and I stole from myself and gave everything to Mekhti, but it was never enough.

I always thought if I just did enough to help, he would see how indispensable I was and the difference between his relationship with me and with his wife would disappear. The perfect servant, that was the one thing she was that I wasn't, and I promised myself I would be that too. When he got thirsty I got him glasses of water, I tore the cupboards apart in search of medicine for his constant headaches and colds, I cleaned for him, I tried to iron his shirts, to cook. But I never knew what to do that he would like. Once I brought him a sandwich with meat and cheese together, the way we make them at home, and he took one bite, then spit it out. Don't you know this is a very serious sin? I'll have to pray for God's forgiveness now. He flung the plate into my lap. The harder I tried, the more mistakes I made and the more trouble I caused him.

He had me walk up and down on his back for his backaches. Something he had his four-year-old daughter do for him before. My wife is too heavy, he said, though I couldn't imagine it because I had gone through all her clothes and she seemed smaller than I was.

Twenty-four

In the beginning, he was always promising to introduce me to his wife, when she and his children got
back, even if I didn't want to be introduced to her.
Everyone loves my wife, he said, as if that meant I
would too. I was afraid of her. I refused to see photographs of her, to open her drawers except to look at her
clothes in the closet. I liked him telling me about all
his other girlfriends but I did not want to hear about
her. Maybe I was afraid I would find something to like
about her and that would complicate my feelings for
Mekhti. Terecita's questions for me were, How can
you do that to his wife and kids? And for him, How can
you be so sinful and call yourself religious?

Throughout the evolution of our relationship he
went to temple almost every Saturday. Even if we had
been up entertaining friends until five in the morning,
he went, bleary-eyed, four hours later. And I stayed in
the apartment and played with his things, feeling lonely
and not a part of anything. I begged him and begged
him to take me with him just one time. Are you crazy,
he said. Everyone there knows me. What would they
say if they saw me with you? But after several weeks
he conceded, providing he drop me off some blocks

from the temple, that I walk in alone and find my own
place. I got as far as through the doors to the lobby and
hung my coat up when I caught sight of him among a
group of men and started to follow him through the
doors. He motioned for me to go another way. I didn't
understand. He came to me discreetly and said, That's
the door to the balcony. Women sit there.

I opened the balcony door. Attendance was sparse,
maybe fifteen women, almost all of them over sixty.
There were one or two younger ones and one girl
maybe twelve or thirteen but she was very dark, like
a Mexican, and it was obvious she didn't speak English. All the women were in long skirts. There were a
few elderly American ladies in polyester suits but
mostly they were very foreign, the kind of old people
from other countries with seamed, tight-lipped faces
and scarves covering their heads, who are pictured in
magazines weeping over sons killed by totalitarian
governments. The men's section looked more lively.
There were little boys running around and all the men
had white prayer shawls over their shoulders and
skull caps, some glinting with gold embroidery, on
their dark heads. Mekhti sat in the front among a special group, chosen because they knew all the prayers
and all the songs in the service and could sing from
beginning to end.

When I came in all the women around me were standing so I stayed standing too, and for me the only variation in the endless chanting was when everyone around me sat down or stood up and I sat down and stood up too. There were what looked like hymnals in the pews and I took one when everyone else did. I didn't realize it at first but I was holding it upside down, because Hebrew books open left to right. After a while I stopped listening to the Hebrew and began reading the English translation in the hymnal. There was something about candles, how candles made from vegetable oil could be lit on the Sabbath but lighting tallow candles was a sin. And I wondered at a religion where so many things were permissible but lighting a certain kind of candle was an offense against God.

When the rabbis paraded around with the scrolls on their shoulders the old foreign ladies crowded up to the front of the balcony to stretch out their fingers with kisses. Everyone was holding out their hands to touch the Torah as it went by, and kissing their fingers, and I did too. At first my thought was whether I would get germs but then I wondered whether I was now Jewish like Mekhti?

He said to me he thought he was incapable of truly loving anyone, that he had never loved anyone, and that is what I remembered when I looked down at him rocking and reciting the Torah with the prayer shawl around his head and shoulders. How can you love God, I thought. How can you live a godly life, keep your covenant with him, if you can't even keep your covenant with your wife? Why, I thought, if you love God, can you not love me?

I used to be religious. I used to believe in God. But when Mekhti came I gave up all the love I had stored up for God to him. I will choose someone close and real over something intangible and unprovable, no matter how tolerant, loving and omnipotent, any day. If only Mekhti could do the same, see God in someone who was so near to him and, as I thought I was, deserving of love.

Twenty-five

I got my learner's permit in November and had been planning on taking Driver's Ed second semester. I was sure I would be the top student. I mean, if all my other classes were easy A's, how could this be any different? How hard could it be to learn to steer a car? The first time my mom took me out, we discovered, shockingly, that I was awful. Not to mention that my mother's shrieks every time I turned a corner or came within five feet of a wall or another car made me a nervous wreck. I had been so excited about learning to drive, so over-confident, but after the first few times behind the wheel I began to dread it as much as my mother did and began making excuses to postpone our practice sessions. By December she had stopped even suggesting them, and I was as relieved as she was.

Mekhti was very impressed that I was learning to drive a car. He didn't seem to care that I was awful at it and hated it. His wife had never driven a car in Samarkand and was terrified of learning. Since there was no one to take me out to practice, he began to take me in his old blue sedan. He was much calmer than my mother, didn't scream when I came close to other cars, and gave me a constant, steady flow of commands. Together we tooled around the parking lots of office complexes and, when I got a little more confident, he began to entertain me while I drove with his own driving stories, of driving into the mountains of Uzbekistan to buy marijuana, of leading a convoy of army trucks through icy passes in the Ural Mountains, of driving a whole truckload of soldiers across a minefield during a practice maneuver, the soldiers playing guitar and singing in back, never guessing what danger they were in.

Winter was very cold that year and there was even ice on the roads. One day he took me out to some back road someplace up near the mountains where it was even colder, to drive on the ice. He intended for it to be fun, like a carnival ride, but I was terrified. The car slipped and spun on the ice and every time I was sure we would crash into the barriers. Mekhti was laughing, steering the car, but when I started to cry he swung the car over to the shoulder immediately. I collapsed against his side and clung to his jacket. He put his arm around me gently. It's all right, he said. I just wanted us to have fun. And it's true that he never once lost control of the car. He promised never to scare me again.

I used to have dreams, lots of dreams when I was little, of riding in the car with my mother driving. And suddenly the car would go off the road over a cliff.

The longest part of the dream was where we would be floating down, like flying but oh so slow, waiting to hit the ground. I would always wake up just before we hit. But it seemed like the actual impact, my death, would be nothing compared to that time in the car, the time when I knew finally I was going to die and there was nothing I could do but wait for the moment to come. That was more awful to me. Once you've stepped off the cliff, or driven over it, or whatever, the torture begins with falling, with the moment you've lost all control. Death can only be salvation, because then nothing, not your helplessness, nothing matters anymore.

Twenty-six

My mother said she did everything because of me. Whenever I complained too much or asked too many unanswerable questions about why things weren't better, she always said the same thing: I did the best I could for you. Leaving Tehran, divorcing my father, marrying Glen so I could finally have a real father, marrying Don although by then, I told her, I was too old for a father. All of it she did for my sake. So why, I wondered, wasn't I happy with her?

I had had more last names than anyone I knew. First my father's which no one could ever pronounce and which I could hardly remember using, then Glen's that was with me practically all my grade school years, then Don's. Whenever someone used my first and last names together I always had to look around like, Is that me? And when, after a long time, I began using my father's last name again, it never sounded quite right. By then it was too late.

When I was little I was curious about everything. I had a game I played with my mother. I would make her stick out her tongue, and I would stick out mine and touch the tip of hers with it. When I got older I was ashamed of having done it, especially since my mother didn't like it. But I think it shows how much she loved me, so much that she did everything I asked, and how for me nothing was ever enough. I wanted to know everything about her, I even knew what her mouth tasted like, and it surprised me and seemed somehow wrong that her mouth should taste different from mine.

Twenty-seven

I was home all day because of winter vacation and my
parents both worked, so he knew that if he called only
I would answer the phone. I was afraid to go out for fear
I would miss it. He would never tell me in advance
what time he would call or what time he would come
over. If I called his apartment there was never anybody there. At first for some reason I was afraid of
letting him know where I lived. I made him meet me in
a parking lot at the edge of my neighborhood. But then
after a while I let him start coming to our house
during the day, when no one else was home.

I wouldn't let him go upstairs to my room. We sat
on the living room couch like opponents facing each
other. When school started again I left the house every
day by a quarter to seven. Around six-thirty or seven
the phone would ring. Sometimes he would say something, sometimes he would just hang up. Especially if
it was my parents who answered, then he always hung
up. I just wanted to hear the sound of your voice, he'd
say later when I'd ask him about it. And I'd say, At six-
thirty in the morning?

Sometimes he would call in the evening too after

dark. We had a system. If I answered before the third ring, everything was okay. I had to hang up the phone if I was downstairs and call him back from my room where I could talk to him without anyone hearing. If one of my parents answered he would hang up, and if I was nearby and heard, I was to go up to my room and call him back immediately. If no one answered by the third ring he would just hang up.

I never knew exactly what time the calls would come but it was always sometime between four and nine at night, four being when he got home from work. I got home from school around three-fifteen, worked on my homework and waited patiently. Then about five-thirty I began to get fretful. I went up to my bedroom and put the phone on my bed, or I sat downstairs in the living room next to the end table that had the phone on it within arm's reach. There I could not only get to the phone if it rang but hear if anyone got to it first and the caller hung up. Most of the time I would sit there all evening. Sometimes I would drift off to sleep. By eight-thirty, when it was pretty obvious he wasn't going to call, I would go upstairs to my room, get under the covers and make myself go to sleep. There was no point in staying awake any longer.

When he did call, he would say, I want to see you. Usually it would be from a pay phone near our house.

He would tell me to watch for him, and when I heard a car slow down outside our house I would slip out to meet it. Or sometimes I would have him park in the driveway and I would tell my mom that Terecita's mom was picking me up. Then I would get into his car and we would go for a drive.

Sometimes he wouldn't call at all but just drive around in hope of seeing me. Even if no one was home but me, and he could tell because there wouldn't be any cars in the driveway, he would never ring the doorbell but instead drive noisily up and down our street hoping I would see him from my upstairs window. If there were no cars outside in the driveway and he saw me walking around in the living room he would stop the car and honk the horn. He wouldn't get out.

Sometimes he would look for me walking home from school. Sometimes he would drive all the way over from where he lived two or three times in one day until he found me at home, if I was late getting out of school or had gone home with Terecita. Sometimes he would drive by my house as early as one o'clock to see if I was home. You know I don't even get out of school until two forty-five, I told him. I know, he said, but I was just hoping you were home sick or had cut class. Once I even found him circling the parking lot after school had let out. What are you doing? I cried. Every-

one will see you! He would just shrug. I needed to see
you. One thing he said to me over and over was, God
sent you to me. God knew we needed each other.

In the beginning I was frightened by the intensity of
his need. I couldn't understand how someone with a
wife and child, a complete family, could need me so
desperately. His wife had left for New York with his
four-year-old daughter only a few weeks before we
met. No grown-up had ever wanted me that badly for
anything, and no one, young or old, had latched onto
me as quickly as he had. People, teachers and kids my
age, usually didn't like me at first. It took most people
months to discover likable things about me. I was
afraid of him, afraid of the inevitable sexuality of our
relationship, yet at the same time I could not let go of
him. I was always making up excuses, even later on
when everything was beyond excusable. That I needed
someone to teach me Persian, that I would forget Persian if he wasn't around. That I would no longer have
anywhere to go outside of home. That no one else
would make room in his life for me the way he had.
And when he began to talk about consummating our
relationship I believed him when he said it would
make us closer. He knew how much I valued his friendship and he told me that without sex our friendship
could not continue as it was. I can't be close to a woman
without it, he said. We can still be friends, sure. But I

won't come to see you as often, maybe just on special occasions, and gradually we will drift apart. That I couldn't bear. I needed to be the center of his attention all the time. If I ever felt like his focus drifted from me, I became frantic. But at the beginning it was hardly a problem. He was always asking me whether he was extra in my life. That was a big issue for him in the beginning especially, because he believed the reason I was always hanging around waiting for his calls was because I was bored with vacation, and that as soon as school started again and I had caught up with all my friends, I would forget all about him. I tried to explain to him that, even then, I knew he meant much more to me, but he said he could not believe it. He wanted me to prove to him that he was needed in my life. It must be by New Year's, he said. Then, by Valentine's Day. Like a present. Sometimes after driving around with me all evening arguing about it he would drive away angry, saying he was in physical pain. You're torturing me, was what he said then.

He begged me to try it, said that I would like it, could not but like it. If not with me, he said, then at least with your boyfriend. My boyfriend to whom I had barely spoken since vacation began. Whenever he or Terecita called, I told them I didn't feel like getting together because I would rather be waiting for Mekhti's calls than risk going out and missing an opportunity to see him. Jason and I had talked about it of course but only that. It was easy to talk as though we were interested in sex when we knew we would never pressure each other into actually doing it. Neither of us wanted to. But the more Mekhti talked about it, the more convinced I became that there was something wrong with me. I thought, I must really want to, deep down, but I'm just afraid of losing control. I hated myself for being afraid. There was no reason not to start doing it. I was not religious. I didn't believe in marriage or chastity. A lot of people my age had already done it. There was no reason not to get it over with while I had the opportunity so that my virginity would stop getting in the way of my relationships with men, like it was with Mekhti. Somehow I thought by going through with it I would be initiating myself into Mekhti's lifestyle. I would make myself his equal and we would no longer be so incomprehensible to each other, he because of his carnality, I because of my old-fashioned fear.

As soon as I made up my mind to do it, I got into Mekhti's car and asked him for advice. He told me long tales about every girl he had ever deflowered and how if we did it right it would only hurt a little, but how that didn't matter because I would want to do it again and again all night and it would be great. Jason was not so confident. At first he was shocked by the change in me, how I had suddenly become so aggres-

sive. Then he was just bewildered. Are you sure you
want to do this? Don't you want to wait? No, I told him.
I've made up my mind.

At first of course I tried to play passionate and pretend that it was him I wanted, he who had brought on
the change in me. But then when we got down to bare
bodies I knew it was going to be a disappointment
and my lack of enthusiasm was difficult to conceal. To
make matters worse, it wouldn't go in. Maybe we
should stop, Jason said. I don't want to hurt you. No, I
said, just push harder. So he pushed and he pushed and
finally there was this noise like a ripping of cloth, and
the pain subsided from excruciating to merely dis-
tracting, and in a few minutes it was over. Jason felt it
was appropriate to hold me. He seemed to think my
offering myself to him, pain and all, was a gesture of
love, although he didn't know what to make of my
coldness. Maybe he thought it was due to shock or
pain. Later we went for a walk, just down the street and
back. Jason was holding my hand, but between my legs
it felt like everything was on fire, and all of a sudden
there was this anger flaring up inside me and I felt like
hitting or biting or kicking someone.

Well, Mekhti asked me, how many times did you do
it? Three? Four? Five? Just once, I said, and it wasn't
what I expected.

After that, I couldn't stand to watch TV. The reason was whenever I saw two people kissing or making love in a commercial, a movie, a music video, whatever, I became physically nauseated. I couldn't listen to love songs on the radio without feeling scorn. It was like a whole dimension of the life I was growing up into had been flattened for me. Anger replaced it. You just weren't with somebody experienced, Mekhti said.

He was always trying to kiss me, fondle me. It was like walking a tightrope or cliff edge. I could not get close to him because just when I began to enjoy our friendship, to laugh at a joke or enjoy a moment shared, he would reach for me to pull me in and I would have to jump back. The first time we kissed, really kissed, was at two in the afternoon at my house. No one was home but us, and we were sitting face to face on the couch, Mekhti telling a story, and I was so absorbed that I leaned forward, and he leaned forward, and our hands touched and held, and something kept nagging me, Go on, go on, and I kissed him. He took off his shirt, stripped down to his sleeveless undershirt, and we came together again. Suddenly he was all over me, rubbing his body over mine, his arms and hands everywhere. Eventually I pushed him away and he left, angry and frustrated. He never wore deodorant, and the smell of his sweat was all over the couch and cushions, all over me. It nauseated me so much that I took a shower and threw the cushions into the washing machine. My mother got mad at me for that later, because they were dry-clean only.

Mekhti was frustrated with me and I was frustrated with myself because there were times I did feel something for him. But it was always when he was away or busy with something else. We would be in the middle of an argument and I would suddenly want him to kiss me. Or I would imagine what it would be like if he were lying on my bed drugged and limp like a doll. But I would never be able to act on my fantasies.

I was fascinated with his naked chest and would beg him to take off his shirt for me. I would have him lie down and would rub his chest in circles and hold up his arms and put my head on his heart, like a doctor listening for a heartbeat, tormenting him. My heels were slipping on the edge, I thought, if I just get it over with, if I give him what he wants, then he will have to give me his body, his man's body.

It happened, of all places, it ended, of all places, in our house, on the couch when no one was home. And it wasn't something I had wanted but then I hadn't struggled either. I had merely hoped it would be like with Jason, that now I would be free to hate him, would

want him no longer. This time, because it was worse, I
ran instead of walking. When he left the house I waited
until I heard his car drive away and then went outside
after him. I ran and ran until I thought I would die of a
heart attack or throw up. It started to rain and the
raindrops burned my sweaty face but that wasn't
enough to stop me. Finally I collapsed in the grass of a
park and I lay there, sky spinning, heart pounding,
hoping to die now that I had done the one thing I had
sworn I wouldn't. Wishing I could keep on falling but
couldn't. My body wouldn't die and the ground was
pressing up all around me. There was nowhere left to
fall.

Skidding on the ice, I am crying and Mekhti pulls the
car over. He holds me gently and says he had never
intended to frighten me, he thought it would be fun. He
never had any intention of hurting me.

Which is what Albert said to me. Often I would go to
him in the morning after Mekhti left for work, if I
hadn't gone to school. Although his work didn't begin
until two he was always up early and dressed no matter
what time I knocked on the door. No matter what time
it was in relation to mealtime he always fixed tea for
me and set out a bowl of crackers or candy. He would
usually be reading when I came in. Chemistry text-
books or some other kind of thick, hard-bound, aca-

demic-looking book in Russian. The only books he
read in English were mathematical treatises and thin
novels for junior high schoolers. Like almost all
Mekhti's friends he'd been here just two years and his
English was hard to understand. But even his broken
English was comforting. He always asked about my
school and then he would slip in something about
Mekhti and me. He was always trying to explain to me
that Mekhti really cared about me, that it was not
what I sometimes thought. That Mekhti would never
intentionally hurt me. But both of us were too embarrassed to discuss it further.

Mostly, Albert's apartment provided a refuge from
my morning loneliness. He would let me watch TV
while he read, as if he were my babysitter. He taught
me to cook, a little. And he wrote my name, first and
last, in Armenian letters, which I pinned to the wall in
Mekhti's bedroom.

Once I asked Albert why he didn't have any kids.
He seemed like he would be a good father, not like
Mekhti. Mekhti might hug and kiss his daughters
when he felt lonely for them, I thought, but when he
was tired or preoccupied he would push them away.
Shut their lonely little faces out of his mind. That, I
thought, explained why he was always saying how his
daughter loved him and listened to him more than to

his wife. Because his affection was something rare and irregular and therefore more valuable.

Albert had been married, he said, but his wife didn't want children. He didn't explain why they divorced.

I often imagined what kind of father Mekhti would be to his girls. I imagined them climbing over his body, walking on his back, kissing him and touching his face with their little hands. He described how his daughter Violeta would run to him when he came home from work, how she deliberately disobeyed her mother all day but would behave as soon as he got home. But I also saw how, if her devotion became too stifling, he would pry her away and hand her to her mother, go into the bedroom to shut himself away. In the middle of the night she would wake up, wander into their room. Papi, I had a nightmare. Hoping to sleep with them. He would carry her back and tuck her into her own cold bed. When his second child, Stella, was born, when he came back from New York, his eyes were bright all the time. He described to me how beautiful she was, how perfect, how tiny. I knew, I know, he loved his family, and that I was too old, too much an individual to compete with those tiny, helpless, innocent creatures. Sitting on his bed, complaining bitterly to him, he said to stop me, Remember you always said you wished I was your father? Did you ever think that was my wish too, for you to be my daughter? But I was the grown-up daughter, independent, unwilling. I would not listen to him, would not yield. Too different, too set, in trying to bend and mold me he could only hurt and break me. I was not full of possibility like the little ones. He could not control my life. In the end he had to let me go.

Twenty-eight

We went for drives together, drives to the mountains,
the lake, the city, the Sound. He liked to drive when he
was bored or when he was anxious and tense. I remember riding in his car, cigarette smoke blowing in
my face, through town after town. We were always
getting lost because I would say to him, Let's go to this
place or that place, then after half an hour's worth of
driving forget how to get there. He asked me to show
him all the really beautiful places, so the first place I
took him was a waterfall. The ride there was long and
restful through gray December fog and he exasperated
me by sneaking his hand onto my leg over and over
even though I kept pushing it off. We followed the exit
signs to the lookout and parked but we couldn't see
anything from the parking lot. You have to walk along
a path and over a wooden suspension bridge to a little
wooden hut and before you even see the waterfall you
know it by the crashing, rushing, thrashing noise it
makes. Mekhti said it was one of the most beautiful
places he had ever seen. But I remember being disappointed because the weather was bad. It was a cloudy
day and had been raining so the whole lookout point
was filled with mist. Everything was grayish white
and you could barely make out the waterfall. All you

could see was the top, gray water disappearing into a
nothingness of white mist. Usually you could see
rocks, the river below. I was in a bad mood after that,
but Mekhti was in a state of exhilaration. He went on
and on in the car about how much it had pleased him
and how even the only bad part, getting wet from the
spray, hadn't spoiled it. How he would have to take his
family there someday. Because at that time he was
always looking ahead and making plans for when his
family came home from New York, places he could take
them, sights they would enjoy, and he liked to discuss
it with me.

But later he went back with some of his own friends,
Garik and Ira, people like that, and when he came back
he was disappointed. It was a clear sunny day in the
spring and the entire waterfall was visible. And it was
so small, he said, he didn't understand why he had
thought it was so beautiful the first time.

Once he told me my fortune. He was always telling
me that he could do it, that he had studied a special
book of magic, the Kabbala, and had learned all kinds
of secrets from old men, old women in Samarkand. He
believed in all curses, spells, love charms and super-
stitions. And somehow his belief in superstition was
tied up with his belief in God, which I didn't quite
understand. He had a string of tiny beads hanging in

his car, black with white dots, to ward off the evil eye. When I asked how you could get the evil eye he said that he personally could get it when a stranger paid him a compliment.

He was always spitting over his shoulder and knocking on wood. Every once in a while he would tell me something like, if you have a dream on a Monday or a Thursday, it will come true. Otherwise it means something about problems you have now. He said if you wake up with a nightmare to go into the bathroom, turn on the tap and recite the dream over the running water. That way the dream would go down the drain with the water, it wouldn't come true. But if you had the dream sleeping on your back, don't worry about it. Nightmares always come to you if you sleep on your back.

Sometimes he analyzed my dreams. Most of my dreams were about him. He was going up the Up escalator and I was on the other one going down and couldn't get over to him. Or I would find myself with a whole group of people who were his family, and I had something to tell him but couldn't get his attention because they were all talking to him.

He told me he had foreseen his own death. Not the way he would die, only that he would die young. He said he had a dream where some person, an angel maybe, came to him and told him his time was almost up. The person said, Soon we will come back and show you how you will die. It upset me and the first thing I asked him was, How are you so sure it was true? Because, he said, I have always been able to see the future and every time I have known when someone was going to die, he died on that very day. He was very afraid of death himself and although he wanted to talk about it he didn't because he said each time he talked about it and especially each time he told someone his future, it took another year off his already shortened life.

That was probably when I started dreaming, daydreaming actually, of his death. It was something I kept coming back to like a scab you pick at until it bleeds. Sometimes I dreamed he was in the hospital, in a coma, and at first I got frightened thinking if it really happened how would I ever find out? Who would be there to contact me? But I thought that I would know somehow and come to see him in the room where his wife and all his relatives were sitting. I would push past them and kneel at his bedside, take his hand and press it to my cheek and the tears would start flowing. And the people would be shocked because they would understand immediately who I was to him, but a part of them would also be touched by my devotion. And Mekhti, lying unconscious, would somehow sense me holding his hand, I had broken through to him because my love was strongest.

Other times I saw his funeral before my eyes, saw the whole room, his relatives all in dark colors, saw him lying in the coffin looking the way he looked asleep, pale and still like he'd left his face behind. But that was where I had to stop, because I couldn't imagine what I would do, how I would act. I thought about it often even though I knew it was terrible to want someone dead. But I was fascinated by the thought of a time and place where I could finally reveal my feelings for what they were and, possibly, it wouldn't matter to anyone.

I liked hearing his stories about the Kabbala, about magicians who, having learned pages, could walk through walls and make themselves disappear. He told me about one magician who was paid a million dollars to escape from a millionaire's mansion before it was blown up with dynamite. It's on video, he said, I can bring it if you want to watch. A crowd of people gathered outside the millionaire's house and the dynamite was lit while the magician was still inside, struggling. Then, in the middle of the explosion, there was a puff of smoke and out of it stepped the magician, about three hundred yards from the dynamited mansion. It's because he studied the Kabbala, Mekhti told me. People who studied it, he said, took years to learn all the secrets in just one page. Only three people had ever learned it all and one of them was Jesus. Jesus was a magician too, he said.

Mekhti said he knew my fortune, and he knew his future including the place and time of his death. Every time he offered to tell my fortune, I refused. I didn't want to know in case it wasn't good enough. But eventually I gave in. It was just too tempting. You'll never be famous, he said. You'll get married twice, and the first marriage will end in divorce but your second husband will be the love of your life. You're getting weaker and weaker, he said, and right now what keeps you strong is your innocence. But at twenty you will lose all control. Why? I wanted to know. Because at twenty, he said, you'll finally learn what sex really is, and you'll lose everything, all your strength, your self control, in pursuit of it. It will be your downfall. I was so angry with him that he told me to forget it, that he had just made it all up to entertain me. I still have the note he left with me the next morning, in apology. But even though I didn't want to believe him I did. He was right that I was growing weaker, and once somebody from the outside tells you something like that, you start seeing the signs in yourself and, once you expect it, it becomes so easy to forgive it when it comes. For five years I believed I felt myself weakening, even after he was gone, and I accepted what I thought my future would be with men, with many men. Only after five years had come and gone and the dangerous age had passed was I able to convince myself that he was wrong, that I would never be tempted by sex, and afterwards my strength returned to me like air rushing into a vacuum. Why did he tell me that? Is that really the future he saw for me? Or could it be he wanted me to become like him, wanted to make me see that I was the same, no better, no worse?

Twenty-nine

He always told me he had never met anyone else like me, there was something wrong with me because I didn't enjoy sex with him. I liked to hear about his other girlfriends in Samarkand, Moscow, Odessa and Minsk. Did all of them like sex? I asked. Did any of them ever get pregnant? One, once, he said. She was a Russian girl, a ballet dancer, and he gave her money because she wanted an abortion. She could have been faking, though, he said and laughed and told me about Russian girls in Samarkand, friends of his, who would get money from their Uzbek boyfriends by pretending to get pregnant. The girls would say, Now we have to get married, and the men, who were very Muslim and could never bring a Russian wife home to their parents, would get scared and quickly cough up five, six, seven hundred dollars for an abortion. I told him, Maybe you have children you don't know about. He admitted it was a possibility. I wondered if somewhere there wasn't some other girl my age, probably younger, some girl or girls in cities across the Soviet Union all looking for Mekhti the way I was looking for my father. He met women when he was in the army, when he worked as a photographer taking pictures of tourists in front of the palaces, when he traveled on business as an antique exporter. Who's the youngest girl you've ever slept with? I asked, expecting he would say I was. But instead he told me that when he was in the army there were Russian girls, thirteen and fourteen years old, who slept around with the soldiers. But they looked older than you, he said, and they were already much more experienced. When I asked him how many women he'd slept with he didn't know.

My favorite girlfriend to hear stories about was Rita. She was the last girlfriend he'd had (not counting one night stands) before leaving Uzbekistan, and when he met her she was sixteen, just one year older than me, which would make her twenty-one when we were to-gether. She was the love of his life and oh so beautiful and she went everywhere with him, to clubs and bars and restaurants. I felt like she was my sister because, like me, she was half Persian (her mother was Iranian and her father, a German, either died or ran off right after she was born) and she lived with her mother and older sister. He told me about how they met. It was at a party, and his friend was seeing her sister. Mekhti saw Rita standing there and asked her to dance, and for the rest of the night he told her such funny stories that she was doubled over laughing. Laughing so hard she had to stop dancing.

I wanted Rita to be like me, but Mekhti said she was

like him. She was fast and tough-talking, something of
a delinquent and known for wild behavior. She carried
a switchblade wherever she went. Once or twice she
saw Mekhti with another woman in a bar or a restau-
rant. She'd fly at the woman, screaming and pulling her
hair, threatening to slit her throat if she didn't stay
away. She wasn't afraid of anyone, women or men
either. Mekhti couldn't count all the times he'd been
forced into a fight because Rita had insulted some man
who'd been eyeing her. She was wild in bed, he said,
and she was crazy about him. But she also really loved
him, they were the best of friends. She even saved his
life once, when he got into a fight in a bar and knifed
somebody who later turned out to be the son of a crime
king. When the crime king put out a contract on Mekhti
and he had to go to Tashkent to hide, Rita went to the
crime king and offered him her body on the condition
that the incident with his son be forgotten. When
Mekhti talked about true friendship it always meant
being ready to help out in difficult and dangerous
situations and often involved some kind of self-sacri-
fice. But he had never been in trouble or needed anything the whole time I'd known him. There was nothing
for me to do or give to prove my devotion. I always
thought, if I just do enough, he'll realize how valuable
I am, how much he needs me. Vacuum the apartment,
do the dishes, massage his back when he is tired. But
what were those things for proving true friendship?

Thirty

When I was little, no one was good enough for my mother but me. Kids would come over to play and we'd paint pictures on my easel. This is for you, they'd say. Later, after they'd gone home, I'd find only my picture hanging. I threw it away, my mother would say. It wasn't nearly as good as yours.

She was so quick to point out the imperfections of my grade school friends. They were too noisy, too nervous and insecure, they were stupid, they broke things. My best friend in kindergarten gave me a tape of her singing Christmas carols for Christmas, probably because her family didn't have enough money for store-bought presents. I played it all the way through, twice, because thinking she had made it just for me was touching, but my mother, when she heard it, said it sounded like a cat yowling and I reluctantly let her throw it in the garbage.

Another friend I had in first grade especially liked my Garfield comic books. One time she borrowed some and was reading them in the car as we drove her home. On the way back, when it was just me and my mother, my mother remarked to me, All she does is look at the pictures. I don't think she even knows how to read. Then she began telling me for the millionth time how smart I was and how I at six years old was already reading at a fourth grade level. My mother had nothing but praise for me, and held such high expectations for me. It was always my secret fear that someday somehow she would decide I was no different from the other children and her reason for loving me would be gone. She spent hundreds of dollars taking me to child psychologists and having my intelligence tested, so there was proof if I wanted it that I was above average. All I remember is a lady in an office telling me to make up a story about a picture she was holding of a family of kangaroos, and I didn't want to, and she was waiting for me, and every time I exhaled loudly she wrote sigh in her notebook and she didn't like it when I pointed out to her that I was not sighing but yawning.

It was always so easy to believe that I was extraordinary. Until I got into junior high and high school and people smarter than me started appearing in my classes. Then I would rush to do something to make the teacher notice me. Tests and assignments made me terribly nervous. Each time I told myself I had to do better than the last and I always felt like I had done my best but it wasn't good enough. Every night from the time a project was assigned until the time it was due I went to bed with a stomach ache. I worried I would not finish on time, I would do a sloppy job. When I finally got my paper back with an A, I felt like I had cheated fate. People told me, So what if you don't get it done on time? Who cares if you get a bad grade on one test? But I knew that even if it was true for them that no one would care, that it didn't matter, it wasn't true for me. Every single paper, every test, every quiz had to be perfect because I was the perfect girl. And I couldn't study too much, either, or else I would be just like the girls who also got straight A's but only because they stayed up doing their homework all night, every night. Getting straight A's because you studied too much was easy, anybody could do that. I had to do what no one else could do.

Not that my mother put any pressure on me to succeed. On the contrary, everything I did seemed to please her. Whenever I brought home a quiz or a paper or a drawing I'd done in school she always exclaimed over it and hung it up or saved it in a special drawer. There is even one memory I have of trying to draw a picture of a dog when I was five and no matter how clearly I saw that dog in my head, on paper it came out all blobby and childish with stick legs. I remember throwing myself down on the floor and crying because I couldn't draw a perfect dog and I remember my mother coming to me and putting her hand on my back and saying it's okay, that when I was older I would be able to draw better.

Why, then, did I always feel like someone was expecting me to perform, to confirm my value over and over by steadily surpassing my own achievements? When I drew a picture, if it was not better than the one I had drawn before, I tore it up. I was so afraid of slowing, of stumbling, it was as though some monster was chasing me all through childhood. If I let it see I was weak, that I was average, then it would catch me and throw me out into the cold. I would no longer deserve to be who I was.

Thirty-one

My high school had a program that gave students Voc Ed credit for community service. The requirement for graduation was one credit of Voc Ed, and since I had absolutely no desire to take accounting, carpentry or Exploring Childhood I signed up to volunteer at an adult ESL school. I rode the bus there after my sixth period class got out and Don or my mother picked me up afterward. I sat with the students, walked around to their tables and explained things they didn't get, photocopied handouts in batches of thirty. I liked it much more than I thought I would. There was one Afghani boy in our class and about twenty people from Uzbekistan and Tadjikistan who spoke Persian. Because I spoke Persian and was the only volunteer younger than seventy I became the students' pet and lots of people asked me for my phone number to call me with questions on the homework and help me practice my Persian. Which is why I thought nothing of it when Mekhti asked me for my phone number at the Christmas party. When he called I picked up the phone right away, because I had been sitting by it waiting for Jason to call. But it was a man with a deep unfamiliar voice, and he asked for me in Persian. Since I had started volunteering people were always calling and speaking in Persian so at first I didn't know who it was. I had already forgotten about the party. With my terrible Persian I asked, as politely as I could, who was calling. I'm Mekhti, the called said, and I remember his exact words. We met at the party, he said, I want to see you. I remember the strangeness of those words. You want to see me? I asked. Why? I just need someone to talk to, was his answer. Can you meet me somewhere?

I remember looking at the clock and thinking, It's seven o'clock and if I don't do this I'll be sitting here, bored, for the rest of the evening. There's a parking lot on 6th and Main, I said. Good, he said, I'll be there in fifteen minutes.

And he hung up. I got up, put on my coat, and went out. I think I told my parents I was going to walk to the 7 Eleven. It was dark, December, and cold, and I don't remember what I thought about as I walked through my neighborhood. Usually, when I walk past people's houses at night I like to look inside their windows. If a light or the TV is on you can see everything. When I got to the corner where I told him to meet me I didn't see anyone there waiting. I crossed the intersection, I thought maybe he had gone into the shopping mall parking lot across the street. I was about to cross back when I heard my name and saw a figure waving an arm at me. I ran across the street, against the light. I thought

maybe you'd gotten lost, I said, and he said he thought
maybe I wouldn't come. As he helped me into his car he
put his hand on my back. I have to tell you, he said,
I'm a little drunk. Actually very drunk. Today was the
anniversary of my father's death.

He got in beside me. Where do you want to go? I
asked. He said, I don't feel like going anywhere. I just
want to talk. I had wanted to go somewhere, to a
movie or to the mall, and I was a little scared to be alone
in a parked car with him in the dark, but I kept my
mouth shut. Maybe he looked harmless to me. Maybe
I didn't want to make him angry by insisting that we
go out. He lit a cigarette and turned towards me. So
you're fifteen, he said. You're in high school? He
asked me to tell about myself. I didn't know what to
tell. He asked me about friends. Did kids in high
school drink or do drugs? Did I? Did I have a boyfriend? Was I interested in talking about sex? A lot of
the questions were difficult for me to understand in
Persian. He had to explain them to me. I can't talk about
that, I said, shocked. I don't even know the Persian
words. A lot of women like talking to me about it, he
said. But I still had nothing to say. Fine, he said, let's go
somewhere. Where do you want to go? I told him I
wanted to go to the mall. We walked around there for a
little while and then went back to his car. He told me
several times where he was from but I remember I

kept confusing Uzbekistan with Azerbaijan. I'm so drunk, he said, you're going to have to help me remember where I parked the car. We found the car and drove back to the corner where we met. I thought it was time for me to go home and reached for the door handle, but he said, No, let's sit and talk for a while. So I sat down again, waiting, but he was silent. I don't know what to say, he said, and then, I want you to be my special friend.

After he had made me his offer I couldn't go back to school the same person. Who else in my class had ever been asked to be a mistress? Because that's what I would be, even though he only said friend. I knew he was married because at our first meeting at the corner he told me that his wife and four-year-old daughter were in New York with his in-laws, that they wouldn't come back until his wife had her baby in April. He told me that he was bored and lonely, the eye of his cigarette turning towards me in the dark. I want you to be my friend, he said. I said I thought we already were friends. I want you as a friend, he said, but I also want you as a woman. And leaning toward me in the car, drunkenly tried to kiss me. I pushed him and he went sprawling against the door, laughed and sat up. At least let me sit next to you. At least let me touch your hand, like this. Don't you want to kiss me? Leaning into me, rubbing his forehead against mine. Why not,

why not? Above us a light came on in the apartment
house, people wanting to know who has been parked
here so long. My hand jumped to the door handle. It's
time for me to go. Just one kiss, he pleaded. I'll see you
tomorrow, I said. Do you promise? Yes, I promise. He
said, I'll call you tomorrow and you can tell me what
your answer is. Okay, I said because I'd already forgotten the question. Although I was standing outside the
car, holding the door, my mind was still inside, feeling
his arm slipping around me, hearing him say, Woman,
you are a woman, I want you as a woman.

I went home to my cozy bed, glad to escape, thinking
he was probably so drunk he wouldn't even remember
what happened the night before, it would be amazing
if he did call, he must realize that I am too young, I
should never have gotten into his car, and with those
thoughts dizzying me I drifted off to sleep.

The next morning I told myself he wouldn't call but
stayed by the phone anyway until eleven when I
couldn't stand it any longer and got up to go for a
walk. I walked all the way to the lake and back although
it was cold and drizzly. I didn't want to come home
but I did because I was hungry and I knew he would
call. And when I got home I couldn't eat because the
thought of putting something in my stomach when it
was this full with waiting nauseated me. The phone

didn't ring all morning. As if it were staying quiet on purpose. I went up to my room and sat on my bed. I came downstairs and watched TV by the phone. It was vacation and I had nothing, no homework or tests, to divert me. I told myself he was probably laughing if he was thinking about me at all, laughing about how he'd scared a poor innocent high school girl. Or, I thought, he was ashamed that, drunk, depressed, missing his father and his wife, he had allowed himself to lose control and fantasize about an affair with the first available female. I thought about calling Jason, my boyfriend, but I knew that with my head full of this new problem I would have nothing to say to him and somehow I didn't want to let him know about it. I thought about calling my best friend from junior high. I wanted to call anyone, someone, only there was no one to call, and I was just reaching to pick up the phone when it rang. How did you sleep, he asked me. I said, just okay, and you? Terribly. He said he had wanted to call me earlier but that because yesterday was the anniversary of his father's death he had to go to the synagogue and pray. Have you thought about my offer? I told him my answer was still no. Your answer is no for now, he said. The Persian made it sound more complicated than that and I made him explain it to me. You can still change your mind, he said. Then he said he wanted to see me today. As long as it's in daylight and lots of people are around, it will be safe,

I thought. But he said that he was busy until five. We met in the same spot. No matter how early I arrived, he was always there before me. He was sitting in his car smoking a cigarette. I got in and he handed me something that had been lying on the dashboard. It was a video from an X-rated video store. Let's go there, he said, and we went. I had never been in a porn shop before. I had gone past it but thought the name, Adult Toys, meant something like cellular phones and radar detectors, or little golf games or wave machines you could set up in your office, like they had in Sharper Image catalogs. I couldn't believe we were really going in. It seemed to me places like this had an over-eighteen age qualification. The guy behind the counter looked at me, probably because I was the only girl in his store. There were men all over, white men, Asian men, young men, old men in suits and ties, picking up videos and looking, putting them back. I followed Mekhti through the aisles as he picked up every other video, saying, This one was good, this one was boring, this one was stupid. I feel sick, I said, let's go. We drove back to our corner and he tried to kiss me again. I reached for the door and this time he grabbed my arm. Let go of me! I said and he did, immediately. He was sorry. He promised that he would never hurt me, that other men would definitely have taken advantage but that he wouldn't do anything unless I wanted him to. I have to go, I said. It's late. Just let me kiss you, he begged. Almost out of the car, I pulled back at the last second and kissed him on the cheek. It was warm, prickly. Then I jumped out. Goodbye, I said, and as I ran I heard him say, I'll call you tomorrow.

He told me later that what drew him to me was how for the longest time I would not let him even touch me. Other girls, the girls he'd known, had all gone to bed with him in a day, three days at the most. His friends, he said, thought he was absolutely crazy to pursue a girl for two months. You're like a magnet, he always said, something inside you pulls me to you. I always asked, What? What is it you see in me? But he could never say. There's just something about you. Like it was me, something in the very center of me, like nothing in any other girl before me. Even later, much later, he couldn't give a reason for his attraction to me. Just that it was there was enough.

Thirty-two

Whenever I stayed the night at Terecita's house, her mom would bring us a plate of tortilla triangles with melted cheese on top. We would sit in her room on her bed and listen to her CD collection and talk. One thing we liked to talk about was the kind of man we hoped to meet when we were old enough. We would have long discussions about whether his hair would be long or short and what he would do for a living. Those were the only times I could almost pretend Mekhti was not happening. I would stay up half the night with Terecita describing the bases to me and the next Monday, after school, Mekhti's car would be waiting for me to go back to his apartment. But that was just in the beginning. Afterwards, I couldn't talk about him very much with Terecita. And as for describing the bases, she couldn't tell me anything I didn't know already and I had nothing I felt comfortable telling her. When I did talk about Mekhti it was in a different way. I complained to her when he was too pushy, too critical, too demanding, when I wished he would leave me but didn't know how to get rid of him. We talked about Mekhti and Terecita's mom's boyfriend at the same time. Each of them was often an interfering, unwanted presence in our lives. But like me, Terecita complained about the boyfriend only sometimes because he had been with them for so long, eight years, that she wasn't sure what life with her mom would be like without him.

Terecita's relationship with her mom was very different from mine. I always tried so hard to see similarities because it seemed like our situations were almost identical. But Terecita and her mom didn't have that same closeness I shared with mine. They were nothing more than mother and child, one person providing care and the other receiving it. Terecita always admired my independence. How if my mother was not at home I could cook a whole meal for myself, wash my clothes, make my bed. I wished I could be like her, as simple as a child. My mother and I were much more than that. I was also her sister, her husband, her best friend. Complaining to me about the narrowness of other people, she would always sigh and, putting her hand over mine, say, You're the only one I can really live with. If it weren't for you I would just live alone. Maybe it was because I was part of her, maybe it was growing up so close to her, but I felt as though no one else in the world was as much like us as we were like each other. Always my mother told me, Other people don't understand. They don't live the way we do. No matter how hard I searched, no matter how much I struggled, I would never find anyone who would be as close to me or understand me as well. I envied Terecita because she was just a daughter. I was my mother's twin, her lifelong companion raised to the role, and no matter how much I hated it, no matter how far away I went, who I said I was, how I reinvented myself, I would always be her mirror image, the person she created to complement herself.

Besides boyfriends our favorite topic of conversation was elementary school. We would spend hours recounting the friends we had, the clubs we made, the games we played, the cartoons we watched on TV. Terecita divided her life into two parts, before fourth grade and after fourth grade, when she moved to her present house. Before fourth grade she moved around all the time, just like my mother and I did, so her memories were mostly of eating cereal and watching cartoons on the living room floor, same TV, different apartments, and of getting in fights with kids in different schools. I liked to hear about after fourth grade. She could tell me long stories about adventures in the woods outside her neighborhood, friendships made and broken, and she could tell me about the most popular people at our school when they were nine, ten, eleven years old and not popular at all. For us, memories of childhood, the books we'd read, the shows we'd watched, the foods we'd eaten, were very sharp and clear. After that, everything became a confused blur. When we were in high school, for some reason, acting immature became cool. We watched cartoons, blew soap bubbles at school during lunch, played on the swings and monkey bars in parks. Things we would never have done at eleven, twelve years old, we were much too grown up then. Terecita and I got out my old Barbies and dressed them up, giggling at the old clothes almost a decade out of style.

One thing Mekhti did not understand about me or any American girls was the effort we made to be silly. Fifteen-year-old girls he knew in Samarkand were quitting school to find jobs or husbands, dressing up in high heels and short skirts. Rita at fifteen worked as a hairdresser in a beauty parlor. He liked to compare me with other girls, both American and foreign. You're so wise for your age, he said. Sometimes you even act older than me. But why do you like such silly things?

I remember him pushing me on the swings. It was the first full day we spent together, the first night I spent at his apartment. We went out early, driving around, and ended up downtown, where we walked through the expensive stores. I took his arm, I liked the way people looked at us together.

Sometimes, though, other times, I felt stupid with him and when he tried to touch me in public I pushed him away. Once when he tried to kiss me outside a

movie theater I tore away from him and ran into the
bathroom. I didn't want him touching me like I was his
girlfriend. That was later, during the last days. I made
lots of scenes then, I didn't care what people thought.

That afternoon we went to a park with tennis courts
because I had been on the tennis team the year before
and had been telling him how good I was. He had never
played tennis. I taught him the rules and how to hold
the racquet, how to serve. He was a match for me even
though he was sixty pounds heavier and eight years
out of shape, and we laughed as we raced around the
court, dusk falling. Afterwards, worn out from playing, I went and laid down on the grass, so cold it felt wet
on my bare skin. Mekhti came over and lay down on
top of me and we rested like that until I heard some
people coming and said, Stop it, you're crushing me.
We left the tennis courts and went down a series of
wooden stairs on the hillside to where the swings and
the playground were. I got on and started pushing
myself higher and higher, so high that finally all I
could see was blue sky. I thought the ground wouldn't
even be there when I looked down. Mekhti dashed in
front of me, back and forth, under and around my feet,
making me afraid that I would hit him. When I jumped
off, finally, it felt like I was flying feet first into the
sky. Mekhti went on the swings too but only after I
begged him. It's for children, he said. My four-year-old

daughter likes it. He didn't really know how to swing.
I had to push him, which was difficult, he was so heavy,
and the ropes twisted. When he jumped off he stumbled
around like a drunk, making funny faces so I would
laugh. One thing he always said, he loved to make me
laugh, to see me happy. Sometimes I would get upset
and cry in front of him and instead of talking it out
with me, of letting me have a good cry, he would tell me
story after funny story until I forgot about being sad.

When we got back in the car I directed him to the
lake. We got there just as the sun was going down.
This park was empty and everything was quiet except
for the plash of the water. So beautiful, rose and blue,
city lights just coming out against the gray horizon,
mountains in a tight ring around the city and, behind
everything, like a beautiful flaming crown, clouds
that were pink and orange. I stretched my toes sitting
on the dock and savored the perfect sunset, the perfect
end to a perfect day shared by two friends. I looked at
Mekhti and he was frowning at the waves beating the
stone steps and he said, Look how dirty the water is.
How can people go swimming in this. I made him sit
down next to me at the edge of the dock. A small boat
went by and even it was rose and gold with the sunset.
The closer we got to the water and the waves, the
colder it became. I held onto Mekhti's arm. All the heat
I felt was coming from him. We sat there until it got

MEKHTI 153

completely dark and then Mekhti took me home. Going down the hill to my house in the middle of Febru-
ary I thought of summer. Of going swimming in the
evening and coming home after dark wrapped in a
towel, of roller-skating and playing basketball in the
street, all the things you do in summer when the evenings are warm. We pulled into my driveway and he
stalled the car. My parents are gone, I told him. They're
gone to the beach for their anniversary and won't be
back until tomorrow. You can stay with me, he said.
Just get your things. We drove the long drive back to
his apartment in the dark and when he unlocked the
door and turned on the light it felt like a holiday. I
bounced on the couch and turned on the TV, old
Popeye cartoons. Mekhti made some scrambled eggs
and came and sat down beside me. We went over the
usual grim topics in my life. School, my deteriorating
relationship with my ex-boyfriend Jason, my parents,
home. Then we went into his bedroom. And of course
it hurt, and he was so heavy on top of me I couldn't
breathe, but I liked the feeling, and this time I concen-
trated and tried so hard I thought I felt something else
too. Like the presentiment of a feeling before the feeling comes or like the husk of something from some
faraway time, a memory somewhere in the back of my
head so that at the very end it felt like my head was
exploding with tension. At the end he always held me
by the shoulders and looked straight down into my

eyes, and this time I grabbed his shoulders too, pushed
my face into his soft neck. This time I was glad we did
it. I think it happened this time, I said. I think I really
felt something. Mekhti looked into my eyes and clicked
his tongue no. My ineptness and inability to feel what
I was supposed to feel was something we had already
had long discussions about. He said I was the only
woman who was not wildly moved by his lovemaking
and he didn't understand why I didn't like it. There
must be something wrong with me, something icy in
my nature, and I agreed for lack of a better explanation.
Whatever necessary nerve endings or neurotransmit-
ters other women had just didn't seem to exist in me,
because I felt nothing, absolutely nothing except sore-
ness afterward. Usually I would complain when Mekhti
began pawing me. I don't want to, I would say. I still
have homework left to do and I can't study when I'm
sore. Or, when he would roll on top of me in the
morning, I have to go to school. How do you expect me
to sit all day long after? But there was only so long I
could run away from it. I do everything for you, he'd
say. Just give me this one thing.

In his bedroom he taught me how to smoke a cigarette. I liked the smell it left. He said he had a way to
show me the future, it would be in the form of shadows on the wall and we would just need some candles,
water and vinegar, but I said no, I didn't want to just

yet. He said his back was sore and asked me to walk on
it for him. I had never heard of such a thing. It's okay,
he said, my wife does it and she's heavier than you.

Afterward he turned out the light but I couldn't
sleep even though it was way past midnight. I couldn't
close my eyes on the sight of him lying there, face
pressed into the pillow, couldn't shut out the sound of
his breathing. Sleep seemed like a waste of conscious-
ness when he was there, so close beside me. I wanted to
wake him up to tell him how much I loved him, but he
was fast asleep. When I touched his fingers they closed
around mine. I hardly ever saw him this way, so quiet.
I thought that I would stare at him all night. I don't
remember falling asleep.

I thought, No girl has what I have. At night in the
dark I would ask him questions and he would answer
sleepily, his voice muffled by the pillow. And I
thought, This is what it is to be married. Having your
husband talk to you in the dark. Do you talk to your
wife like this, I asked. At night, in bed? Where do you
think we discuss all our problems? He said. It was one
of those questions you ask knowing the answer but
hoping it will be different. How could they be married
eleven years without her once hearing his voice sleepy
in the darkness from the other side of the bed? But
still I hated imagining her curled up against his back or

him against hers, like two spoons together every night
of their married life. I hated her innocence, her ignorance, believing in a monogamous husband, in the
bliss of marital fidelity, never guessing somewhere
across the country was a girl that would have killed her
to talk her place. Mekhti said, you have no right to be
jealous. I never gave you any reason to believe I did
not love my wife, to believe I had any intention of
leaving her for you. Once he came right out and said it.
If you ever do anything to break up my family, I will
make your life a living hell.

So I burned in silence. My fantasy was that his wife
would die. Her death might be painful but at least I
would wish for it to be as quick as possible. Some
possibilities were a car crash in New York, a plane
crash coming home, a stabbing in Central Park, or that
old favorite, dying in childbirth. So when Mekhti described her to me as fragile and petite I silently cheered
inside. If she died, I thought, his daughter and the baby,
if it survived, would come to live with us. His daughter would be like my little sister and the baby would
grow up thinking I was its mother. I imagined how I
would befriend four-year-old Violeta, draw her pictures, play games with her, take her to the zoo. I would
give her American-sounding nicknames like Vee instead of Violeta. Maybe I would even love her more
than Mekhti.

It frustrated me that I did not know what his daughter looked like but about his wife I didn't want to know.
I prevented him from showing me any picture of her,
even her passport photo. There was a picture of both of
them together on the refrigerator that I tried not to
look at. I asked Mekhti to take it down, which made
him angry, but he let me cover it with a blank sheet of
paper, under the magnet, so that I wouldn't have to see
it. After a while, especially after he came back from
New York, I think he was glad the picture was not
there for his eyes to see. Like me, he was forcing
reality to split down the middle into our secret life
together, just the two of us, and our lives apart with
other people. The problem was that as time went on it
became easier to push out the other people from our
private life but harder and harder to exclude thoughts
of each other from the everyday world.

Things were so tangled and confused I thought they
would never come to an end, which is why it came as
such a shock when he called me from the airport. His
bond to her was stronger after all, and I knew that he
would forget all about what had happened between us
as soon as he saw her again in New York. I hated him for
being able to involve himself so deeply with me and
then slip away so easily. There was nowhere to go, no
future now. It was as if time stopped. How, I wondered,

would he get my things out of his apartment before
she came back? Albert would clean it up, I supposed.
He would take down my name in Armenian, he would
tear it up. I could have gone back to him to talk, but I
was incapable of talking to anyone. My most precious
refuge was sleep. I went to bed early, crashed like I was
exhausted, and on weekends I slept until eleven or
twelve o'clock. I would wake up, look through the
window outside, and close my eyes again because
there was absolutely no reason to get up. I didn't eat,
hoping if I didn't fuel it my body would just naturally
wear down and die. I went to school every day for the
first time in months but inside I was empty or dead.
People who asked got told the truth, that I had broken
up with my boyfriend, but it was so strange and
simple it felt like a lie.

At night I dreamed of fire, of self-immolation. I
dreamed of all of us, him, me, his wife, perishing in a
raging fire. Dreams were the only time my mind came
alive. During the day it shut down. Whatever electrical
impulses passed through my brain only took the form
of words, no pictures.

But it was just five days, and then the phone rang
and he was back. No explanations. Simply, she had had
the baby and decided to stay. And I moved back in and
we went on living as we had before. Except something

had changed in him. Something had been defeated. He
stopped talking about her, telling me how wonderful
she was. I stopped caring about the end. He kept finding reasons why she shouldn't come back yet, that his
job wasn't going well, he didn't have enough money
saved, the weather would be bad for the baby. And
aside from missing him, she liked it in New York. She
said every place else was boring.

He called and said simply, I came back. The baby had
a cold and his wife had to stay there a little longer.
Within a day I was back at his apartment, even though
I had told myself I didn't want to be there. He had
ended it once. Why go back only to end it again in a
week, a month, two months? But after a day or two I
stopped thinking about endings because all that mattered was us, now, together. I kept on going to school
regularly. I only missed one or maybe two days a
week. The late-night parties had stopped. Whenever
Mekhti's friends called, the ones that came with cham-
pagne, vodka and weed, he told them he was busy. We
spent the evenings alone together talking or, more
often, I would read and do homework and he would
sit next to me on the couch and watch TV. He didn't
understand anything of what I was doing except the
math (math, he said, was his best subject and the only
subject he paid attention to in school because it re-
quired no studying) but he said he liked me near him.

And afterwards when we went to bed it would be quiet and perfunctory. I sort of knew now I would never enjoy it. All the things I had hoped would get better I quit thinking about. I just looked up at the ceiling or off to the side and he stopped asking me how I felt after. He had changed too since he came back. His wife's family must have had feasts every night in honor of the baby and his visit because he came back several pounds heavier, and he had me resew the buttons on all of his pants. His friends teased him about his belly, saying, Now it must be your turn to have a baby. But he hardly ever talked about his baby or his wife. Before, in the beginning, he told everyone who would listen, me in particular, about the baby coming in New York. But to me at least he never mentioned anything about his other life there after he came back. I think that he was trying not to think about it. I think that before he had seen the baby's arrival as a natural end to our relationship but now that his wife had decided not to come back he realized it was not so simple. Really it was up to him when to end it. He could postpone her return indefinitely or he could have her back right now if he wanted. The trouble was, he didn't know what he wanted. There was always some new reason why she couldn't come home. And at the same time he told me I had to make my own choice. It was up to me to leave. This relationship isn't healthy for you, he'd say. It's interfering with school (as if he

had only now realized it), with your relationship with
your parents. I'm torturing you, was what he said
over and over again.

Whenever he worried like that about me I would
throw my arms around him, count the ways he had
changed my life for the better, say things like, Without you I couldn't be happy. And he would look at me
with eyes full of glad amazement. Eloquent words of
love could not move him, but sometimes I would say
something so simple, some little thing, that would
make him so grateful. In the dark, in the middle of the
night, I would wake up and he would be lying on his
back, eyes open, and as soon as I moved just a little he
would pull me close and rub his face in my hair, holding me so tight I could hardly breathe, and whisper,
Don't ever leave. But I had changed too and the more he
said those kinds of things to me the harder it got to
answer him. When he left, I thought that was the end.
Something inside me, the part that lived just for him,
that part died or was killed and something else was
moving into its place. Something less fiery, less bril-
liant, but stronger, calmer. It was something even I
didn't understand. Before, he was like loaves and
fishes to me. No matter how much of himself he gave
to me, it always seemed as if there was more and I
wanted it. Before, I could not get my arms all the way
around him. Now it seemed like there was not enough

of him. A few minutes after and his skin was pale and
cooling, his legs already cold. I wanted to use myself to
cover him and make him warm again.

Thirty-three

My SAT scores came back in May but I didn't tell
Mekhti. My English teacher brought me brochures for
student summer programs in other states. A summer
program at Harvard for high school students. A quarter at MIT for kids interested in science and engineering. Summer research opportunities for kids who
wanted to be doctors. Programs for building schools in
Iceland, churches in Chile. She told me, You have to get
away. You have to go out on your own or you'll never
find out for yourself what you think and what you
want. You're too young to have people forcing their
values, their reality on you.

When I first thought about leaving, it made me sick.
I thought about how difficult it would be to separate
from my mother. How even if I wanted to I could not
leave Mekhti, not if there was hope of even one more
day together with him. I knew that. Leaving him would
be like dying, like murdering myself. And if I had to die
in order to live, I wasn't strong enough or brave enough
to do it myself. Someone would have to bind and gag
me, carry me off. But I knew I would not struggle.

My English teacher was so sure of what was best for

me that she phoned my parents, and she filled out the application while my mother wrote the essay for me and they sent it off. So I found out in May that I was going to California for the summer but I didn't tell Mekhti. I couldn't believe I had done it.

Thirty-four

Before the baby came we would hold each other tight at night and in the morning. I would squeeze his hands white and cry because the end was near. Sure, I could forget sometimes, but whenever I looked up it would be there. The end.

After she came back from New York that intensity, that frantic insecurity was gone. Because we realized what was keeping us together, what could tear us apart, was not his wife and the birth of his baby, not anymore, but our own wishes in our own hearts. He would come home from work and go straight to the bathroom or the bedroom to avoid me because whenever we sat down together there would be a long talk of Why don't you leave me? Why can't you leave me? Why don't you do something? He would say, Why do you stay when I torture you so? And I would say, I can't leave you, you have to make me leave. And he would say, I can't.

He complained that I pressured him although we both knew I had no right and that I tried my best not to. When I asked him what he meant by me pressuring him he said, It's that I'm incapable of hurting your feelings and I'm unable to refuse you anything. It's tearing me apart but I can't not do what you want. I want to be with you and I want to be with her too. Couldn't we all just live together? He was only half-joking.

Before, when I told him what I wanted, he got angry and said cruel things to stop my thoughts. He'd say, If I tell her, and sometimes I want to, then neither of you will ever see me again. I'll have to go away, I couldn't live with either of you knowing one of you was the reason I lost the other. I couldn't be happy with you if I knew that because of us, my wife and children were unhappy.

And he'd slam the door, go off to Edik or Nina or whoever understood him better than I did, leaving me alone in the cold apartment that was not mine. I could have gotten on a bus and gone home but I always stayed and waited for him to come back. He was always back by morning and he would be sorry and hold me on his lap, and I who had been furious all this time would start crying, and he would say, Don't cry or I'll start crying too, and tell me he would never leave me.

Thirty-five

In the dark I am lying with him, my head on his arm. And he is only half-dressed because there is never any time, because, he says, he will have to get up and leave soon. So I press against that arm as close as I can knowing that no closeness will ever be enough. He's as close to me as he will ever be, his sharp smell, his skin, his fingertips, but already every atom, every particle of his body is swimming away from me and I'm waking up from a nightmare screaming, one where you dream you can't breathe because you know, you know it will all be taken away. Holding him tight and not looking at him it's like I can see, I know this is not mine, it cannot last, and always in slow motion behind my eyes, like the movie you can hear but cannot see as you step into the theater darkness I can feel him going, leaving. And I hold tighter but he does not know. If only he would ask me, What are you afraid of? Then I could tell him. I feel it sometimes, feel it so much, I would die to be with him, when he is gone sometimes I am so miserable I want to commit suicide. This empty aching like he has gone and taken the whole world with him and I am left in this vacuum. Alone. So that when he comes and lets the world in again there is so much around me. Like a whirlwind, it knocks me to the ground.

Thirty-six

That semester they started a new program where classes were shortened and a new last period was added on each day called Tutorial. Students could go to the teachers and get help in their most difficult subjects. And during that time, I started hanging around my English teacher and together we worked through different problems. I couldn't really tell her about the past or the present but we worked on the future, how I wanted to live my life and what kind of person I wanted to be. Instead of telling me what I was she was asking me, Are you strong, do you want to be strong? I hated that word, strong, after what Mekhti said. I'm weak, I told her. Every day I get weaker. You're fettered, she said. It's your chains that are growing heavier. Once we set you free, you'll see how strong you are.

The drama club was holding auditions for the play they were going to put on at the end of the school year. She wanted me to try out for the part of the villain. But I can't act, I said. I can't pretend to be people I'm not. But she thought I would succeed marvelously, she said, and when I told Albert he thought so too. I told Albert before I told Mekhti because it seemed like another betrayal. The first thing Mekhti said when I

did tell him was, But when will I see you? Because
rehearsals were after school. But then he seemed to
reconsider and said it was good for me to get back into
school activities again and that he would pick me up
after rehearsals so I wouldn't have to take the bus in
the dark. I didn't really like the thought of his junky
old car, one fender dented because he didn't have the
money to get it fixed, waiting outside the theater
every day, where everyone could see, but it was better
than waiting for the bus.

Thirty-seven

For my birthday in May he took me camping. Albert
was coming and Nina to keep him company and Mekhti
told me we would drink beer and play music and
dance in front of the campfire and have lots of fun
after the sun went down. I had never been camping
before. I had never known anyone who knew how and
who could take me. It was something Mekhti always
promised me, whenever things were going badly he
would remind me that someday, as soon as it got
warm, we would go camping in the mountains.

There had been warm weather for days now and I
was really excited to go. Early Saturday morning we
went out and bought everything we needed. Hot dogs,
tomatoes, cucumbers, bread, charcoal, beer, plastic
forks, chocolate. Mekhti had borrowed the tent and
sleeping bags from someone earlier that week. Albert
was bringing the fishing poles. Nina was supposed to
meet us outside the building at one. When we had
waited half an hour, Mekhti and Albert went into
Albert's apartment to call her. They came out looking
angry. She's not home, they said. When I asked where
she could be, Mekhti said probably drinking somewhere. He asked Albert if he still wanted to go, and

Albert shrugged. Why not? They had left a message on Nina's answering machine telling how to get to the campsite. Albert said he'd go in his own car so he could go back early if it didn't work out.

We got into Mekhti's car and I sat behind the driver's seat, my arms around his neck, chin on his shoulder so I could see all the way out the windshield. It was fifty miles to the campsite. We drove over valleys of trees, past waterfalls and mountain slopes that were still covered in snow. There was a lake with a small dam, a cabin, a train trestle with a chunk blown out of its middle on stilts among the trees. We drove higher and higher, past the ski resort, all grass and brown earth now. We took the wrong exit and had to turn around. The forest road into the campsite was long and winding with several turnoffs onto dirt roads. Mekhti asked me to read the signs for him because they were in English.

We got there exactly one hour after we started. Mekhti and Albert parked the cars by the river. The first thing we did was pitch the tent and unload the groceries. Then we had to gather wood for a fire. I was surprised at how much wood it took for just one fire. Mekhti had us scraping all over the campsite and in the woods for branches while he and Albert told stories of their army days. Afterwards we sat on logs and

ate cold sandwiches and tomato and cucumber salad,
waiting for Nina. Not only was it cold but dark, too,
because the trees were so tall. We all had our jackets
on. Mekhti brought out the beer and he and Albert
took turns standing and toasting me. We hope you
will always be as beautiful, as fresh, as sweet a girl as
you are today.

Mekhti reached into his coat pocket. I have a surprise
for you! My heart sank because I knew what it would
be. He brought out his pipe and a packet of weed. He
and Albert took deep tokes and Mekhti blew into my
mouth from his. I didn't really want to, already I was
cold and this would just make me colder, but Mekhti
said, Come on, it's your birthday.

Someone was fishing in the river at the campsite
next to ours and Albert said that he was going to go find
the lake and try it there. Mekhti got up expecting me to
go too but I shook my head. The weed was already
working on me and I wanted to be by myself. When
I'm stoned, I just want to curl up in a corner and think
about how alone I am. If other people are around me, I
get mad at them.

Mekhti pushed me to join them but he seemed to
understand something wasn't right, and they left. At
first I thought I would sit in the car with the heater on

to get warm, but then I thought it might be nice to take a walk down to the river. I scrambled down the stones and sat for a while, and the drug and the cold and the twilight made the river roar, made me close my eyes and listen and let it rush over and over me. I heard so much, listening to the river, that it seemed like I could sit there and listen for ages.

I don't know how long I sat. Ten, twenty minutes, half an hour. I was stiff and even colder when I got up. I stumbled on the stones, dizzy as if I'd just woken up from a dream-filled nap.

I wandered back to the campsite, sure Mekhti and Albert would be back by now, but no one was there. I walked down the road to the lake, which I still hadn't seen. Here, the sun shone through. I sat on a grassy knoll and looked out on the lake that was like God's mirror, huge and flat and glassy, with gigantic mountains all around. This time it was the silence that spoke to me, the kind of windy silence you hear only in wild natural places. Where, if you listen, you can hear the emptiness. Not the trees or the water or the mountains but the empty spaces all around telling you how big everything is, how small you are.

I looked all around for them, in every open place on that side of the lake, but they were nowhere. So I went back the other way, past our empty campsite and the other campsites until I came to the little cabin where the park ranger stayed, and I climbed a hill there, and I went back again. Just as Mekhti's car came into view, I heard voices calling me.

Mekhti came toward me, almost running, his face severe. We were looking for you, he said. Didn't you hear us calling you? We were looking for you for over half an hour.

I could have gotten lost, he said. Fallen into the river and drowned. He told me to never run away from him again, and I said I was sorry. It was easy to say that now that all my wanderlust was spent.

Nina still hadn't come, and Albert said he had had enough. He was going home. Besides, he had noticed the overnight fee for two cars was double the fee for one. He wished me a happy birthday again, got in his car and drove off. Mekhti shrugged.

By now it was completely dark. Mekhti built a fire while I watched, carefully arranging layers of moss, twigs, then finally branches crisscrossing over the top. He lit it carefully and poked it, stirred it and blew on it until it caught. Making fires, he said, was something he learned to do well in the army.

It seemed like the whole camping trip for Albert and Mekhti, everything about it, reminded them of their days in the army, and they sat on logs and reminisced about camping out on the steppe, shooting rifles and lighting fires in the snow, making me feel like I was very young and they two old men. All the while complaining how cold it was here.

Mekhti lit the fire and we sat down on one of the logs. Other campers around us had fires too. They were all that could be seen in the dark.

All day long campers had been staring at us as we talked and laughed and argued loudly in Persian, and I had stared back. On my walk I had looked into each of their campsites. All the same camping gear, the same nylon tents, but so many different kinds of people, different faces gathered for one purpose in one place. A group of young men, roughing it for two or three days. Kids my age driving in for a party, one car for each couple. But mostly they were families. A little boy and his mother playing Sorry on a tree stump while the dad cooked dinner on a portable stove. We should have brought board games, I thought to myself, or at least a pack of cards. This family must go camping a lot.

Families in RVs, dads sitting in lawn chairs while little girls raced around on bicycles. Directly across from our campsite was a young couple in sweats moving around in front of their tent. Of all the people, including the kids my age, they were the ones that interested me the most. The girl was blond, her hair tied back in a ponytail, her boyfriend or husband looked preppy. They had everything you could possibly want for camping plus a shiny new Lexus. Watching them, I suddenly wished I could change places with that girl because her life was meant for me. Where would I be when I was twenty-five, twenty-six, twenty-seven? Who would I be with? Turning back to Mekhti, he looked old and sleazy and tired.

We sat in front of the fire and warmed ourselves. Mekhti took my hands in his and rubbed them. I watched the sparks float up into the sky and the paper wriggle like blackened worms as the fire ate it up.

Now it really felt like the whole world was just the two of us. It was so dark that beyond the fire there was nothing. In the city, where there were always street lamps, car headlights, porch lights, lighted windows, it was dark but never like this. This was absolute.

Mekhti took my hand. Things had eased up since Albert had gone. Once I stopped thinking that it was my birthday, I stopped feeling guilty for not enjoying myself. I listened to the fire crackle. An ember blew onto my sock and burned a hole in it. I must still have been a little stoned because I just stared at the hole in my sock and felt the sting of the burn.

Eventually we were the only campers with a fire still burning, and our fire had almost burned itself out. It took so much wood for just that one fire, I wondered how much it would take to survive an entire night in the cold forest if you were stranded alone. I read that the best thing to do in a situation like that is to find a rocky wall or fallen log and build the fire next to it. Then you can sleep with your face to the fire and your back to the wall, to keep the wind off. But what if there is no wall?

When ours was the last fire burning, Mekhti got up and said it was time to go to bed. We needed a flashlight to find the tent. It was ice cold, cold like snow. We got under the layers of sleeping bags and held each other. Taking off our clothes, even our jackets, was unthinkable. Mekhti said he had never seen such weather in May anywhere except in Siberia. I know how we can make ourselves warm, he said.

I was too cold to relax but it did heat my body. He held onto me, shivering, but soon I was so warm that I had to take off my shirt. I was so hot I couldn't sleep and I held him all night and rubbed his back, his

shoulders, anything that was cold. It was my job to keep
him warm. She kept me warm all night long, he told
Albert later, when we got back. She was as warm as an
oven.

When I woke up in the morning it was brilliantly
light outside and two mosquitoes were buzzing in the
ceiling of the tent. I thought it must be at least nine but
Mekhti woke up too, looked at his watch and said it was
only 6:30. He got up and groaned, his bones creaking
like an old man's. I was cold but other than that felt fine.
I put on my sweatshirt and used the restroom facility
while he started the fire going again and cooked us
some eggs.

After breakfast I asked him to go for a walk with me
to get warm. We walked past all the campsites until
there were just trees, as tall as any trees I had ever
seen, and signs indicating more campsites off other
roads to the left and right. We crossed over a tiny
bridge and there were more trees.

Walking made me happy. I love walking in the
woods, I told Mekhti. I wish we lived near a place like
this. Mekhti said he didn't like being in nature, that
was the difference between us. He liked people, I
liked being alone. Now I really see how different we
are, he said. He sat down on the ground, grimacing, and

said his stomach hurt from walking. I was disappointed because I wanted to go on. But Mekhti said he had come far enough for today. It was time to go back.

We had to take down the tent, which was a little sad, and we loaded all the things into the car. Mekhti turned on the heater and was happy again. I was so tired I could hardly keep my eyes open. We drove back in silence and went straight to bed when we got home, without even unloading the car first. He turned up the heat in the apartment, we took off all our clothes and got into bed, and Mekhti wrapped his arms around me and fell asleep instantly. But it was cold there too.

Thirty-eight

When he was away in New York that terrible thing started happening to me where I'd see him wherever I went. It had happened to me before, when I was nine and went to summer camp. I hated camp before I even got there because I could not imagine how I could live in a cabin full of other people. The thought of not having one moment of privacy was terrifying. How could I read at night, how could I sleep, how could I take a shower, what if I had gas? I couldn't live with a group of girls. I begged my mother not to take me and she said, It's only two weeks. I screamed and wouldn't let go of her jacket. She pushed me out of the car and onto the bus.

As soon as I got to camp I started seeing her. One counselor would turn the back of her head to me and it would look like her. I would see her walking around the corner of a building but when I ran after her she would be gone, or it would be one of the cafeteria ladies. I was always mistaking the camp mistress for her because they both had the same short blond hair.

She sent me cards with pictures of baby animals on them every day and our counselor told me she would have to throw me in the pool because I was the camper with the most mail. Girls would come by my bunk and touch my stuffed animals when I wasn't watching. Finally, I fell out of my bunk and broke my wrist and I was glad to go home.

After Mekhti left I saw him everywhere, in every man. I called a surprised Terecita and she invited me to go to the mall with her to return the blue polo shirt her grandma had bought her. Everywhere we walked I saw him. Especially if the man was not too tall, not too thin, with dark hair. Sometimes it was just a leather jacket that fooled me, or a certain way of standing in leather loafers. Or a male head as it turned, black hair receding. All of them were Mekhti but then, when I blinked or looked a second time, it was someone else's husband, father, friend. I saw so many of them that by the time we went home I was ready to cry.

It seemed very important to point out to Terecita someone who looked like him so that she too would understand he was everywhere. Look, I would say, him. Terecita looked hard. She said, He looks like everyone else.

And it became a game. That one looks like my dad. That one looks like my grandma. Everyone the other had never met.

Thirty-nine

I have a dream in which I am running through the woods, looking for someone lost, only I don't know who the person is. I hear his voice but I can't see him and he is getting farther and farther away from me.

I can't stop myself. Like a stream that can't slow down or change course I tumble over sticks over rocks over you. Something is calling me away, turning my head away so that whenever your back is turned I slip away to meet it. My face is turned to the sun, it's so dark where you are. Everywhere I go alone I find beauty. I sit beside the river and listen to the water roar until the sound is inside me. I close my eyes and the water is rushing through me in my eyes and ears and out my fingers and toes. I sit by the lake and move my eyes along the shore and the reflection becomes the sky for me. Everything is a watercolor world, pastel trees streaking into the sky. I watch the flame eat the paper black, watch the tiny sizzling worms. I can't share any of it with you. I have to get away. The way the sun falls on the trees, I climb a bald hill and it is like a mountain top. The farther away, the more beauty. I want to walk away into the water, the trees. And you don't understand. You think I am angry at you. I look at you and you're just a person. You'll never understand. I see you, zipped up in your jacket. There is nothing inside, just old age and emptiness. You are sad the whole time and I don't care. The way you talk about me, push at me, press on me. All the while pushing me away. You say you thought you lost me and I think you did. Who is pushing who away?

I lie with you, I cover your body with my legs and arms because I feel it's the last time. You fit so perfectly against me, so solid and blunt, your head on my arm, my lips at your neck. You never let me go. But it's my heat you need, not me.

We pause to rest and you say I see that we are very different. You thought you knew me. You want to stop and I want to walk on. I would leave you behind but I would also curl up on the trail and die if I could push you ahead of me. You say you woke up so many times and each time I was awake and holding you. I told you, Don't sleep. You're not with me when you sleep, I lose you. I have to let you go, but I hold on, pretending you are awake and with me. If you go away, I will have to reinvent myself. Who will I be if you are gone?

I want to ask you questions in the dark and hear you mumble answers back to me. You say life flows from your veins into mine. When I am full you will be empty. Both of us can't be at the same time. I want to lay you down and put my mouth on every part of your body. But it never happens in real life. Once I held you and I heard you roar and felt your teeth. I can fit all around you. I can lift you between my legs. Your center is so so small.

Forty

One day he suddenly decided I was grown. He didn't
like me to walk on his back anymore. You've gained
weight, he said. But you were only gone for a week, I
said. How tall are you now? he asked. We went into the
bathroom and I weighed myself and he measured me
from head to foot with a tape measure. I had grown one
inch and gained twelve pounds since the beginning of
the school year. Then Mekhti stepped on the scale. He
had gained only three pounds since his return from
New York.

From then on we checked ourselves every day. I
weighed myself and marked my height against a piece
of tape on the wall and even measured my waist, my
hips, the circumference of my thighs, and Mekhti
weighed himself and counted every hair lost on the
pillow and every hair turned gray. But somehow the
changes weren't satisfactory, they didn't add up to
what we felt inside.

Forty-one

Mekhti was different from everyone else I knew because he was young and old at the same time. Sometimes he could act as young as I was, but he told me that
was because I was much older than my age. The only
thing that really gave away his age was his taste in
music and clothes, and we had lots of arguments in the
car about what radio station to listen to and lots of
discussions at home about why I wanted to dress like a
clown and why he wore cardigan sweaters with pat-
terns like Turkish carpets. Clothes were everything to
him and, I could see by looking through his wife's
clothes, to her too. I had never seen such pretentious
people. Everything had to be gold and silver and fur
and mohair and real leather. Once he went out and
bought a designer suit for six hundred dollars, what he
paid each month for rent for his apartment. I guessed
there was some kind of rivalry among his relatives that
made it important who owned the most furniture,
bought their first house or was first to work in an
office. It was the one thing I understood, and scorned,
about him.

When he came back from New York there was a
videotape of the party they threw after the baby was

born. I didn't want to watch it until he assured me his wife wasn't in it, she was still in bed with the baby. There was a huge red velvet casino, chandeliers and a crystal bar, an immense table laden with ice sculptures, fruit, melon baskets, cold cuts and canapés, a white cake in the shape of a carriage, the camera panning nine feet of it at least. Dancing and several hundred dark-haired people kicking their heels and jangling their bracelets. Mekhti tossing wads of money into the air for the musicians, dancing on top of it. And one little girl dancing in the middle, her rear end sticking out, giggling and clapping. His four-year-old daughter, Violeta.

He said it had taken him two years to save the money, five thousand dollars. What about savings? I asked. What about investments? Your children's college?

He said, You Americans don't know how to live.

Forty-two

Mekhti talked a lot about his father who had died two years before in Israel from cirrhosis of the liver. His father was the only person he truly respected, and I could tell he admired him because often, when giving me advice, he would repeat something his father had said to him. I could also tell how close and complex their relationship was by the stories he told, how in one story they were dear friends, in another bitter enemies, how his father was so strict with him because he thought he knew what was best and how Mekhti hated him because he thought he did too. How each would have died for the other and each would have been validated if the other did die or was killed, because neither could understand how the other lived and why he acted the way he did. I couldn't understand all of it, not knowing the Persian words, but I felt it because it was the same between me and my mother, that kind of vicious tooth-on-bone love that makes people tear each other apart, makes total opposites tear each other down to find out what keeps them separate. Mekhti and his father, in my imagination, were like two snarling animals circling, they could not get closer without killing each other, but if they both turned and walked away their hearts would break. Mekhti's father carried a grudge because Mekhti was not the son he wanted him to be, too wild, too angry, too irresponsible, maybe too much like himself at sixteen, seventeen, and Mekhti both hated and adored his father because his father could not give him the love he believed he deserved. That was what I imagined. Or maybe that love took the shape it did because his father was often away on business when he was a child, or maybe because he died before Mekhti had a chance to prove his love. Maybe it wasn't what I thought. I always wanted to make everyone into me.

But Mekhti never talked about his mother. I knew only two things about her, that she spoke Russian and Persian fluently but not Uzbek, because it was beneath her to haggle in the bazaars, and that once, when she caught Mekhti's father with his mistress of many years, he beat her so badly she had to go to the hospital.

Mekhti said he and his father were a match because both were proud and stubborn. He spent nearly all of high school living at friends' houses because either his father threw him out of the house or he himself walked out during a fight. Once it was smoking cigarettes and he didn't come back for a month, another time it was for smoking pot. I could picture both of them in the living room screaming at each other, the mother in the kitchen pretending nothing was happening. They probably never hugged or touched each other, maybe because their feelings were too strong. One touch and they would burst into flames or eat each other up.

I could tell that Mekhti wouldn't have been the same person without his father. For me it was my mother, not my father. Remembering what I could of my childhood, I couldn't think of a thing my father personally, not his family, not his country, had done to direct my life. Besides disappearing, like a tooth you don't notice until it's gone and nothing is left but the smooth salty hole.

I thought of Mekhti's mother as a frail old lady in black with white hair. She was probably frightened to be living all alone in the big house with her eldest son (not Mekhti) nearby but not near enough. She probably sat up in bed at night with the light on, trembling, afraid that every shout, every crash outside was a gang of Muslims breaking into the house. Her son probably brought her groceries during the day and her son's wife probably sat with her and held her hand. But Mekhti, when I told him, laughed and said his mother was as tough as he was and even if she didn't speak Uzbek she could swear in Persian the same as anybody who spent their whole life in a bazaar.

I made Mekhti's mother into the same person as my

grandmother and became obsessed with finding out everything I could about her. My fantasies were to get rid of his wife, adopt his daughters and be adopted by his mother. What would she think of me, I was always asking Mekhti. Do you think she'd like me? He had told me she really liked his wife (everyone fell in love with his wife at first sight). If she liked his wife then she probably wouldn't like me, since his wife and I didn't share the same qualities. For so long I was obsessed with her, fantasized about being her daughter-in-law, granddaughter. Would she like me? I asked Mekhti. He began to laugh. You better pray she never finds out about you, because she would make your life and mine a living hell. She would blame me, he said, for tempting him away from his wife, and she would never forgive me. And she knew magic, real magic, because she hung around with the really old people who knew the Kabbala and, he said, that meant she really could make my life hell. After that I was sorry I ever dreamed of loving her.

I wondered what my own grandmother and aunties would think of me now, after all I had done. I had wanted so badly to find them, but was it fair to let them see what I had become? I asked Mekhti, would they ever be able to understand? Of course not, he said, they would think just like my mother. Do you have a grandfather, he asked. No, I said. Well, that's good, he said, because if he was anything like my father he would have killed you for what you've done with me, for bringing shame on your family's name. I asked him why, then, had he done it to me, and he couldn't answer. He said, But this is America. Your stepfather isn't going to kill you for sleeping with me, is he?

The shame I felt started to interfere with my life everywhere, at school, with teachers, in conversations with strangers. Adults would smile while they talked to me and I would think, If they only knew what I was doing last night they would despise me. Part of the guilt I felt was for fooling them. It was all I could do not to run away from everyone.

I didn't know what kind of thoughts I should have in my head. This was the time when Mekhti was asking me, Do you like Ilya? Would you sleep with Abram? What about a foursome? And on the street I would look at men with one thought in my head, what it would be like to sleep with them. I hoped that, to please Mekhti, I would feel something, desire, interest, lust, but I didn't. I knew I could never go through with it. All I felt was afraid and I knew if that person I was looking at now, walking along in his hat and coat, was standing above me naked I would throw up or scream or cry. What was wrong with me that it wasn't fun?

Forty-three

My mother never spoke to any of her family, to any of my aunts, uncles or cousins. She didn't like them because they were richer than we were or poorer or smarter or stupider, she wanted them all to be like her. She wanted me to be like her too. She was half French and she always told me when I was little that I looked just like a little French schoolgirl. She told me that I would be beautiful, that I would be a model. When I was eleven or twelve I began to realize that the person I was growing up into was not the person either of us wanted me to be. I really believed in that girl, whoever she was, that tall, slender, golden young woman, the model, wearing the fur coat and driving the expensive car. That girl who could be an actress, a writer, a scientist, a Nobel Prize winner (nothing was too good for us). I really believed that someday she would emerge. I waited for her as long as I could and so did my mother, and the moment we both realized she wasn't to be was when my mother turned away from me, when she became preoccupied with Don and her second marriage.

We both tried not to notice the real me that was emerging, the awkward, straggling, shy girl. My mother would look at me, her chin on her bejeweled hand, and she would smile her smile and look at me like she was looking into a mirror, not really paying attention to what she was seeing, or maybe imagining more than she was seeing, and she would talk to me and go on talking, looking and seeing something else entirely. I would feel like shaking her, yelling, This is who I am, look at me, look at me. You wouldn't really notice that she did not see until you heard her talking about someone and realized that her descriptions didn't match the person at all. About someone really kind she might say, He is so superficial and narcissistic, and she might call a cold egotist the most caring person in the world. She could call blue eyes green, brown eyes blue. I have brown hair, and she always told strangers, My child has the most beautiful golden brown hair, always insisting that my hair was golden, golden until I wanted to scream. I felt like shouting, Does it really matter? No matter who she saw, what she heard, in her mind it became only what she wanted to hear, what she wanted to see, as if she were trapped inside a room of mirrors that reflected only herself. I became terribly insecure when I talked to people. When I was answering a teacher's question, telling a story, giving a report in class especially, I would panic, I was so overwhelmed by the possibilities of alternate perception. I would choose my words so carefully until there could be no doubt, but still, who can say that the words meant the same thing to others as they did to me? Who can say that the people hearing did not hear something completely different or something that made no sense at all? The same thing would happen when I looked at my face in the mirror. It sometimes seemed to change before my very eyes, now beautiful, now ugly. Who could say what other people thought it was? The longer I spent alone, the more everything around me seemed to gel. I knew who I was and I was strong. But I would look into other people's faces and falter, I never knew what I was to them. After a school vacation, after two or three weeks of living inside myself, it was such a shock to come back, talk to people and hear myself misunderstood so often.

Forty-four

The school play opened in June, just a couple of weeks after my birthday and the camping trip with Mekhti. He came to the opening night but I rode with my parents. I was afraid that when I got on-stage I would see him in the audience and lose my composure and so I tried hard not to look out beyond the stage, but when I finally did all I could see was a sea of darkness and blinding light. I stopped spending the night at his apartment, saying I had finals to study for. School was over the next week, I told him I was leaving for a summer program in California and wouldn't be back until August. He said he understood. On my last day at home we went out, went downtown, walked on the waterfront, bought hamburgers and ate them over the railing looking down into the water. We walked by a store with a rack of summer dresses out front and I reached out my hand to touch them. Do you want one, he said. I'll buy it for you. The next morning by eight I was at the airport. He called me twice in California. Once to say I had made the right decision, we were better off apart, and the other time, the last time, to say he missed me more than anything in the world and he couldn't stay there any longer, he was moving to New York. You don't care, do you, he said. I couldn't say anything.

When I came back in August I took a bus to his apartment. I couldn't believe it was true that he was gone. I went up to his apartment and rang the bell. I rang and rang and rang but it was empty. I went downstairs and knocked on Albert's door. It was morning, so he was home. He seemed surprised to see me. Mekhti didn't think you would come back, he said. Did you look for him upstairs? He moved back to New York in July.

Did he leave me anything, I asked. No, Albert said, he wanted to leave you his phone number but then he said it would be too hard for both of you if you called him. He said he hoped you would understand.

Forty-five

I was sick a lot that year. Maybe it was because we
had such a cold winter, maybe because I never slept
enough and Mekhti was always giving me his colds.
He was always sick too because, he said, he wasn't
used to our wet, cold climate. He went around in long
underwear under his clothes and never opened the
windows. I caught lots of colds from him, maybe five
or six that year. The worst ones were when his friends
came over constantly and there was always cigarette
smoke in the apartment. At night it would make my
throat sore and I would lose my voice the next day.
Sometimes I would lose my voice for a week. That,
partly, was why I avoided going to school. I got sick the
last week of winter vacation, but this was a cold I
caught at school from forgetting to wash my hands or
chewing on my pencil. It wasn't a head cold, just a
general weakness and achiness and then a fever. When
Mekhti came, when my parents were at work, he
brought me bouquets of carnations from Safeway and
told me jokes and funny stories about the times he was
sick, how his family avoided the Uzbek doctors and
bribed the Russian medical school professors to treat
them, how his appendix ruptured when he was thirteen
and he had to go to the hospital and the surgeon was

drunk. When his mother saw the surgeon and realized what state he was in she threw such a tantrum that they called in the chief surgeon, a professor, who performed the operation on the spot. His stories were hard to understand but no one had ever brought me flowers before, pink and red. I put them in a glass jar on the floor of my room until they wilted and turned brown. I had never had my own bouquet of flowers. And he played Middle Eastern melodies on our piano and sang songs in Persian that echoed through the house. He told me that having a fever makes a person aroused. We were sitting on the couch. He asked if he could kiss me. I said no. He asked again and I said no again. He asked, What do I have to do for you to let me? I said nothing, it was impossible. I'll let you kiss me, he said. I was silent. What if I don't wait for your permission? I'll push you away I said and demonstrated, hard. Say I don't know again, he cried, say yes say anything but no. Later, much later, he told me it was because he really didn't know any better. He said, I've never met a girl who really meant it when she said no. All girls who say no really mean yes. He explained it was like a game. It excites them more, he said, to pretend they are afraid. I wondered how well he really knew all the women he'd seduced, all the one-night stands. Maybe I wasn't the only girl who was honest, and he simply couldn't tell the difference in the heat of the moment. I asked him and he said no.

He was no rapist.

I even had a cold next to the last week in April when he called me from the airport and there wasn't enough time to go to say goodbye. This time it was a sinus infection that made the rest of the week seem like a daze. It was one of those things that feels much worse than it is and I went to school every day, ran home in the rain, didn't eat. I wanted it to kill me. I thought I was dying. By the end of the week I had a fever. My voice was so listless when he called that he must have thought I didn't care, and he didn't even mention me coming back to his apartment. He said he would call me again soon and hung up. But my fever was calming in a way. My face was pink and warm and it felt like something was baking inside me, like bread in an oven. Baking and humming. That week Terecita and I went to the mall, and I remember thinking afterwards, maybe my seeing him everywhere was because I was sick. Maybe it was a sign I was delirious. As soon as he called me and gave me the news he was coming back, I sank down into the couch and fell asleep and in the morning, when I woke up thirteen hours later, I let myself stay home from school. Either my mind was empty, or it was too full of things to think about, but for the moment there was no need to run away from my thoughts. Everything could wait while I rested.

Forty-six

That whole week without Mekhti I slept in my own
bed in my own room. My room was clean, no clothes
on the floor, no papers on the desk, since I was hardly
ever home. Nights were so hard. The first time I stayed
the night at Mekhti's apartment I thrashed around and
stole the covers from him and in the morning, when
he woke me up, he said, you're not used to sleeping
with another person are you? But here I woke up on the
same side of the bed I fell asleep on, in the same
position, curled up on my side. My room in the dark
seemed so strange, like a room in a hotel, my bed so
wide and empty. I slept on my side with my fists under
my chin and my feet tucked under me, and my feet were
always cold. I tried to avoid brushing against the other
side of the bed where it was even colder. My bed was
our bed, in his apartment, a double bed that could have
been wider, with its warm rumpled sheets smelling
like cigarette smoke and bodies. The pillows smelled
like the shampoo he used. I couldn't sleep in my own
bed anymore, and I would lie awake at night, listening
for sounds I couldn't hear. More than anything I missed
my mother. I wished that I could go into her bedroom
and wake her up and hug her. When I was little, when
my father left, my mother would sleep with me every

night. She would get into my bed with me and rub my back until I fell asleep. After my mother got married to Glen, my stepfather, she stopped sleeping in my room and started sleeping in her own bed, with him. When I asked my mother, she said it was because Glen didn't think it was appropriate and besides, all the books on child psychology said only children who slept in their own beds could grow up to be healthy independent adolescents and that children who slept with their parents were spoiled and would have problems when it was time for them to start school. All I remember is the nightmares I had that year that seemed to go on and on, new ones each night where I was being chased and eaten by huge monsters, spiders, animals. I was afraid to go to sleep and got up to go to the bathroom about thirty times each night. The light in the bathroom was the only thing that made me feel safe.

I wanted to talk to my mom but I couldn't. Once I came into the kitchen and she was eating something over the sink, her back to me, and I wanted to go up to her and put my arms around her but I was afraid of what she would think because I never touched her. I hadn't hugged her since I was eight or nine years old except on certain days like her birthday. I couldn't touch her, and though she didn't understand it any-more than I did, she accepted it and I hoped she wasn't hurt by it. But now I wanted more than anything to hug her, just once at least, and there was nothing I could do about it. There was no way to tell her what my life was like. Maybe she knew. I still doubt she could have ever believed the whole extent of what was going on or guessed it, but she probably knew when I told her I was staying with Terecita I wasn't telling the truth. There were times when I wanted to go to her and tell her, or at least drop hints, about Mekhti and me. So she would know, and sit down with me and have a long talk like we used to whenever I had a big problem, and I could finally breathe a sigh of relief and realize the things I did weren't so bad after all. That there was always a way to mend my life, that there was always a way to climb back up again. But what price would I have to pay for that redemption? What would she think of me, in what little invisible ways would she change towards me? This was not the girl she had seen in me when I was little, this was not who she wanted me to be. I think that from the start she simply tried not to see who I'd become. I think that by following Mekhti I had finally and irreversibly stepped off the path she'd chosen for me. It wasn't deliberate. I had just wandered off, and I was too afraid to tell her I was lost. I didn't want to go back, I'm pretty sure of that. But I had yet to find my own way out.

There was no middle ground. With my mother you either had to be her, be hers, or lose her. I was afraid of what would happen to us if she found out that I had my own secrets. That instead of growing into her I was showing all the signs of becoming someone else.

Forty-seven

You are sitting in his long blue car. Some window
lights above you flick on and off like people are trying
to figure out what the hell you've been doing here for
so long. And you know, you know you should get out
but you want to stay because nothing like this has
ever happened to you before and it's hard to decide
what to do when not a word is spoken in English. He
sits so close to you and all you can do is go, Yes, okay,
and he keeps asking, Can I kiss you? Remember each
time the answer is no. And when his face is so close to
yours, his forehead on yours so warm, you want to
turn around to look but you can't do that. His teeth so
white, his eyes glisten, all of a sudden he is so handsome. He smells like alcohol, breathing on your neck,
but it's a sweet smell. Thank god for the thing clutching
your chest or you would fall right into him. That one
moment he rubs his forehead against yours and whis-
pers, Why not, why not? It's all so awful and then that
one moment, that one moment was so pathetic and
sweet. He is really drunk, just remember. Don't try to
think about how nice it feels, him stroking your hand,
your wrist. When you saw him in the light, his hair all
rumpled, he looked like he'd just woken from a nap.
Admit it, it's so nice when he lets his hand rest on

your back, your waist. You want someone so confident, so sophisticated, so different. So adult. And in
that language it all sounds so beautiful. Except when
he says Woman, then you know he is not sincere. He
is so direct with you, he treats you like an adult. You
want to learn, you want to love someone who can
hurt you. If they hurt you they're swallowing all that
love and spitting it back at you. But swallowing is the
important word, consumption is important. Watching
him speak, wondering what is going on inside him,
not trusting him at all, you like this too much. He is
offering to take you under his wing, be a mentor to
you, the irony is he makes it sound like he is giving
you a place in his life. Patience is the beautiful thing.
Patience and perseverance. And the idea of an affair.
His little hands, his gorgeous, twisted nose. You feel
so grown up and special.

Forty-eight

I hated that word, Woman. He used it in the beginning, before I would sleep with him. You are a woman,
he'd say, you have the needs of a woman. I want you as
a friend and as a woman. Then, later, you are my
girlfriend, that's my girl, I've never met a girl like you
and never will. You're like my little sister, my daughter, my child. I got stoned and laughed and laughed
and he said, Until now I never realized how young
you really are but now I see it. When he came back from
New York, after his second daughter was born, he left
me alone at night. I can't, he said, I mean I can but
afterwards I feel sick about it. Every time my daughter
kissed me goodnight I thought of you and I wanted to
push her away. My wife didn't understand what was
wrong. Now that I am here I see you and think of her.

It was so easy to know what I saw in him but I never
knew what he saw in me. I read in a magazine that
older men like younger girls because they like being
in control, and they like the adoration, it feeds their
egos. But I don't think it was just that. Because why
would he choose me when there were plenty of fifteen-year-old Yulias and Katyas he could have had?
Albert, when I asked him, said the same thing as

Mekhti. You listen to him, he said. Mekhti doesn't tell
his problems to everyone. Maybe it's because I love
him so much, I suggested. No, Albert said, that scares
him. I remember at night, holding onto him, saying,
No one could have loved you this much. And him
answering, You're the third person to have said that to
me. Both my wife and Rita said the exact same thing. I
don't believe it, I said. It's true, she said, my wife says
it to me all the time. She can't love you the way I do, I
said. He gave me a look. My wife and I have been
together eleven years. You've known me for four and a
half months. Who do you think loves me more? He
went on to say he loved nobody, he had never loved
anybody like women had loved him, so much that they
turned their lives upside down for him. His wife trying
to kill herself, Rita trying to kill other women, and
then there was me. He wondered if there wasn't something wrong with him, if all the weed he'd smoked
hadn't killed all his feelings. To tell the truth, he said,
I've never loved anybody that much.

If he said it all just to hurt and discourage me, it
worked. I lay on his chest, my tongue like a block of
wood in my mouth, wondering how I was going to
cope with all these feelings inside me for a person who
not only couldn't reciprocate them but couldn't even
begin to understand them. I always wanted to ask him
about love. How much he loved me, who he loved best,

me, his wife or Rita. He refused to answer me. I told you, he said, I can't compare you all. Do you love Rita or your wife more? I asked. He started to protest but I interrupted, It doesn't have anything to do with me. It won't make any difference in our relationship. Please, tell me. He hesitated. He said, Her. He put his hand on my lap, between my legs. Who? I asked. Her, Rita or her, your wife? He just said Her again. I told him I didn't understand. If you don't understand, he said, then you don't understand anything at all.

He didn't want to talk to me about his feelings or about love, he said, because he didn't want to do anything to make our relationship worse than it already was. By worse he meant my becoming even more attached to him. But always, after we'd made love, he would whisper, Do you love me? Each time, until finally I told him to stop. You know the answer, I said. Why do you have to keep hearing it? And in front of his friends, Ilya and Abram and Garik, whenever he introduced me to someone for the first time, he would ask me, Do you love me? I always hated giving the answer in front of other people.

Forty-nine

I got the part in the play. I was the villain, the jealous
wizard who captures the beautiful fairy and keeps her
from the hunter who loves her. I loved reading from he
script because I could laugh and act wicked and it
didn't matter what I felt like inside, whether I felt the
same or differently. Rehearsing my part without the
script was more difficult because I was very stiff, and
I think the drama coach began to have second thoughts
about choosing me for the part. Every day after rehearsals after school I would come home and spend
hours practicing my lines in the bedroom while Mekhti
was watching TV. Mekhti stayed in the other room
while I rehearsed because he said it made him nervous to hear so much English spoken right next to
him. I made him read through the other parts in the
script so I could memorize my lines. He stumbled
through the parts of the hunter (Where has love gone?)
and the fairy (True love never dies) in his broken English and quit when I laughed at him. He didn't like the
play because it took up so much of my time. For me it
was the only thing about school I did like. I liked joking
with the other people in the play and making friends
with them. Everyone had a nickname, a stage name,
and they gave me one too. I had never had a nickname

before. I would burst in the door after Mekhti had already gotten home and was cooking dinner for himself because there was nobody else to do it, and I would begin telling him this thing or that, all excited, the words flowing easily from having talked all afternoon, and he would say, Can't we talk about something else for a change? He didn't like hearing about the people in the cast. You're way above them, he would say. Why do they interest you so much? When I said anything about the boys in particular he would tell me to cut it out, they're all just kids.

Fifty

I didn't notice the people who really cared. Jason, Terecita, the teachers who made so many allowances to get me through the year. For me being loved was never enough. I couldn't respect people who just loved me. There had to be some bite and sting, some pain there too. Some people love you so easily. All they have to do is look at you once and the decision is made. But love like that is just too simple. I wanted to be able to choose people that I could love, people who didn't want to love me, and make them fall in love with me. Mekhti for example. Throughout my life I would pick one person and focus only on him. No one else mattered, and it was always someone whose back was turned to me. Or someone who couldn't stand the sight of me, or someone who already had enough people to love. By the time I met Mekhti, I had already learned it was rare to find someone with a vacant space in his life, waiting for you to fill it. People always have relatives, they have children, they have friends, husbands, wives, boyfriends, girlfriends. The older the person you choose the more crowded it gets. And nobody ever needed somebody like me.

Terecita was the only one. She hung onto me because

she knew I was like her, shy without people in my life. Being lonely most of the time had made us the same in a lot of ways. Plus our families. It almost seemed like we should be more alike than we were. I wanted so badly for Terecita's parents to be more like mine, so she could understand how I felt about them. But Terecita looked at everything differently. She thought I took my mother for granted and spent too much time thinking about my father. He's not what you think he is, she'd say. I thought she took both her parents for granted, especially her father. He took her skiing in Chile, sailing in the Galapagos Islands. She knew every detail of his face, the color of his beard, the shape of his glasses. Oh, my dad, she'd say, like none of it mattered. But wouldn't you want to look for him if you had never met him? Terecita was too practical. If he'd never kept in touch, she said, it would be because he had no interest in her, and in that case she wouldn't want to see him either. She'd ask, What are you going to do if you find your dad's family? What are you going to say? Are you going to tell them about Mekhti? When she said that I got mad. Mekhti was not a permanent part of my life, I told her, I told myself, not like a scar on my face, not visible. He was more like a dream you have all night long, the whole time it seems like the dream is you, but finally you wake up and can't even remember what it was about. Or so I hoped.

Frail, fragile Terecita had one thing I envied most of all. She was so sure of her body. Looking in the mirror, she could see her long legs were her mom's, her forehead and eyes were her dad's. She took it for granted that she knew both sides of where she came from so that, growing up, nothing surprised her. She could see her dad in her, her mother. She knew how she'd turn out. I had only my mother, and growing, finding myself growing away from her, was like a nightmare of falling. You don't look anything like your mother, people would say. And my mother would say,Oh, you look just like me. She would have liked to pretend I came from her only, like the immaculate conception, and that everything in me was from her. You're smart because I'm smart, she said once, but usually she said it was because of all the books, books she'd bought me, and the time she'd spent with me. I didn't know if my father was smart or not, but I assumed he was. I didn't remember anything personal about him, how he spoke, his gestures, his face. He was just a shadowy figure moving around the places I remembered from my early childhood, and he was always in the background. In front were my grandmother and the aunts and their little daughters. That was something I didn't want to think about. Could you just replace a child? The way my mother always talked I believed it was something women couldn't do but men could. As if when they divorced my mother they divorced me too. And I was supposed to forget about them because fathers could also be replaced. We kept hoping for a better one, like the picky girl who waits too long to get married and turns down all her suitors and eventually finds herself an old maid. Maybe we expected too much. I know I did. I wanted a father who would love me completely and exclusively. I was always asking, Do you love me best? Who do you love best, me or my mom? My mother when I asked her who she loved best always answered me of course. But my stepfather, what could he say? He'd married my mother, not me. I was the trial he endured to prove his love for my mother. The best he could say was, I love you both in different ways. I always saw it as being jealous. My mother loved me best, and he knew it. So he wasn't going to let me win twice by giving me the cream of his love too. I wanted so badly for him to love me, I tried so hard, my mother's love didn't matter. And sometimes I was so exhausted by my want that I would scream and misbehave and we would end up hating each other. I just wasn't strong enough to make him look, notice me, I wasn't old enough, interesting enough, didn't have anything to offer for love. Sometimes I wonder if he thinks about me. If he wonders about this woman and the little girl whose lives joined his so briefly. He can't have forgotten us. You can't forget something like a marriage. I thought about finding him. What would we say to each other? There were

so many people I wanted to find. A whole list of
people that had gone out of my life, more than had
come in. There was my father, my grandmother, the
stepfather Glen, my aunts and cousins. Jason was my
first boyfriend, would I ever want to find him someday? And Terecita, who really did move at the end of
the summer when her mom got the new job in Nevada. And Mekhti. I'd never had any kind of relationship or known anyone, a friend, a relative, a teacher,
for more than a couple of years. It was always just me
and my mother, running to and from people. If I
hungonto a friend at school too long my mom would
say, Aren't you a little tired of her by now? She hated
me for being more gregarious than she was, for not
being bored by other people. Only you never bore me,
she'd say, her chin in her bejeweled hand, gazing at
me. But deep down I knew I wasn't any more worthy of
her love than any of my grade school friends, Julie who
was always too thin, Jenny who bit her nails. I wondered if it wouldn't be better to tell her, so that she
could give it to someone more deserving. It felt like
stealing. With Mekhti it was similar. I felt bad that I
couldn't enjoy what we did in bed, even though I
tried so hard to feel something. He knew it was an
ordeal for me. Especially toward the end when he
slowed down long enough to look into my eyes, and it
made him nervous and angry. I felt like a thief, loving
him so much, clinging to him so hard when I couldn't

appreciate that act that meant the most to him. There must be hundreds of girls, I thought, who would enjoy it. Like Rita. Rita who he loved most of all because she was most like him, and enjoyed sex, and enjoyed a fight, carried a switchblade in her boot and was not scared of anything. But opposites attract, he always said.

The last time we met, we stood on the pier, our elbows on the railing. I was looking out over the Sound, at the ferries crossing to the islands, while Mekhti was just staring into the dark water. You know how I feel about you, was all he said. And all I said was, Yes. It had gotten too painful. Painful to be with him, painful to be separate, but worst of all was this slow tearing apart. We both knew at that point that it would never be over until we ended it, and that until we ended it our lives could not begin. His wife would come back, they would be a family again. He had to be there for his daughters. When, once again, I had asked him to compare his love for me, he'd said, Maybe I love my children just a little bit more. That's why I have to choose them over you. But although he could say he had made the choice, he couldn't go through with it. Every week I prepared myself thinking this was the week his family would arrive. And every week there would be some new excuse, and I would listen without really hearing. One week he couldn't take it anymore and when he came home from work he told me, She's coming back next Sunday, I've already reserved the tickets. I didn't say anything, didn't even look at him, and he said, You don't care, do you? I either shook my head or shrugged, I don't remember which. He got up and left the room. But that Sunday she still didn't come. And when I left he was still alone. When he called me in California, the first time, he said, Your name in Armenian letters that Albert made for you, I still have it folded up in my wallet. I've missed you. The second time he called to tell me they were all together again and moving back to New York. I asked him, My name in Armenian, do you still have it? And he answered yes.

Fifty-one

He always spoke to me in Persian, never in English. But what I spoke depended on my mood. If I was happy I spoke Persian, my voice and hands excited and fluttery, like a young bird learning how to fly. But when I was mad at him I spoke only English, to make him work to understand me. He still answered only in Persian.

After a while, Persian became my excuse. And I knew it didn't matter but I kept telling myself that it did. I told myself that without him I would forget Persian. That I was learning it through him. As if he were the only person on the planet besides me who spoke it. Sometimes, when I wanted something to blame for what had happened to me, I blamed myself for learning Persian. I would never have met him if I hadn't learned Persian, if I hadn't been so interested in finding my father. Those afternoons in my room diligently copying out Persian grammar from a library textbook or, even earlier, learning to write the letters correctly, how to dot the vowels, I never would have guessed what it would bring me. It was just a memory game, serious but impractical. I never thought I'd use it. I just thought, This is my language, I want to learn it. I wanted to have it inside me even if I was the only one who knew. Later, hearing it actually spoken, hearing how people told dirty jokes, swore in it, it was never the same for me.

Fifty-two

I will always think it was my love of the exotic that did me in. Not being content with the American side of my family, wanting to know more. Learning Persian at home when at school we had either French or Spanish. Even when I was in middle school, I would get out atlases and maps from the library and imagine myself in other places, even other times. If I had stayed put I would have been safe. You can't go from one life into another. If you do, you end up dragging the old life behind you. And you can't bring other worlds into your world without unleashing monsters. It will change you forever so that nowhere is home, everywhere is a foreign country. And if by some cruel twist of fate, someone forces you out of one world and then into another, and another, it's best to forget all but the present. You can't live in more than one dimension simultaneously.

Fifty-three

By the end I was just going through the motions of finding them. My heart wasn't in it. You can't pull people in and out of your life, I learned that from my parents. If they had wanted to find me, I concluded, they would have found me. I had heard on TV and read in books about private detectives who could find missing family members but when I called one in the phone book he told me it would be eight hundred dollars just to start looking in California for my father and when I said the word Iran he told me just to forget it. Try the Red Cross, he said. So I phoned the local Red Cross. An elderly lady answered the phone. I tried to explain that I was looking for members of my family, very close members of my family like my dad and my grandmother who were somewhere in Iran and could the Red Cross help find people like that? The lady said, Oh dear, in that way elderly people have that makes you feel like you've frightened them, and then she said, I'll transfer you to Social Services. Another woman answered but she sounded younger and much more professional. This time I said everything a little differently. I told my story as though I was doing research for a report on the Red Cross and I wanted to know, hypothetically, if family members in America

wanted to get in touch with family members in another country, say Iran, would it be possible? She asked,
Was it a U.S. military family? I said no. Was the sepa-
ration due to a war or natural disaster? Kind of, I said,
and I explained how some of the family members who
were now in America had had to leave because of the
war. She said she wasn't sure what kind of services
the Red Cross offered in Iran and she made me wait
while she looked it up. She came back saying the Red
Cross had pulled out of Iran in 1988 on account of the
war but still operated via the Red Crescent Society
which was a kind of Muslim Red Cross. They had
been responsible for releasing and repatriating 140,000
prisoners of war. Could your family be prisoners of
war, she asked. I said no, I didn't think so. What I can
do, she said, is send you a form to fill out and then
send it to the Red Crescent in Iran, via Red Cross
National Headquarters, to do a trace. But I can't promise anything. How does that work, I asked. The Red
Cross, she said, will search its computer database for
people who have contacted the Red Crescent Society
in Iran. I asked, So if somebody in Iran knew somebody in America was looking for them they could come
to this Red Crescent to get in touch with them? She
said, Yes, the Red Cross has an international message
bank. I asked, And if these people's relatives in Tehran
had tried to look for them earlier and had gone to the
Red Crescent Society, the people in America would
have heard about it? Yes, she said, Red Cross Headquarters would have contacted you and

have heard about it? Yes, she said, Red Cross Headquarters would have contacted you and sent you the
message form they filled out. Would most people in
Iran know about that? I asked. She said she didn't
know, but since the Red Cross is a worldwide organi-
zation and the Red Crescent is Iran's own Red Cross,
most people should know about it. You would have to
be very isolated, she said, not to know about the Red
Cross. When I hung up I realized she had said nothing
about my hypothetical family, she'd known all along
it was me. And now I knew for sure that they hadn't
tried to find me, not ever. Still, I waited for the Red
Cross to send me their form, but it never came. Then I
realized I had given Terecita's address, because I didn't
want my mother to know about it. Terecita's mom had
probably opened it and thrown it out, not knowing
who it was for.

They hadn't looked for me, if they were still in Iran.
What were they thinking, if they were thinking about
me at all? That I was happier without them, happier
as an American? They probably thought by now I had
been converted to my mother's attitude, afraid of
foreigners, ashamed of them. Were we just too hard to
find? Wherever we lived our phone number was un-
listed. But whenever we moved we always left a for-
warding address. Did my mother purposely try to
prevent my father from finding us? Did she hope he

would find us?

By that time I realized finding him wouldn't change anything. It wouldn't change who I was, who I would be. But if I changed myself, then I could learn to live without people falling in and out of my life. That is how I thought at the end.

Fifty-four

When I imagined an ending it never involved him
directly. I would run into someone who had known
him. Not Albert, although we tried to stay friends
after, when I started going to community college the
next year through Running Start. But it was too hard.
He would tell me, drop by any time, I'm lonely. And I
would call him on the phone and we would run
through all the pleasantries, how are you doing, how
is work, how is school, how is your health, and then
there was nothing to say. We never talked about
Mekhti, but he had been what bound us together. I
went to visit Albert once or twice but it was hard, his
apartment looked just like Mekhti's, and then when he
moved it still wasn't easy, I was beginning to forget
Persian and there was only so long we could sit there
and eat candy and peanuts and smile embarrassed
smiles at each other. It was someone else I had to run
into. Nina, the woman whose high drunken laugh
woke me up at night, who had kissed my ear with her
tongue. We walked right by each other in the shoe
department of a big department store and I didn't
recognize her, but she recognized me. I would never
have known her the way she was now. I didn't really
remember how she was before, but someone looking

the way she did now could never have been part of
Mekhti's crowd. She had put on weight, she was wearing casual, expensive clothes. She had married an
American, she said, and had settled down. It was too
late to have children, but she had a step-daughter.
And they had just recently bought a house. Her American husband didn't want her to work, her job was to
stay at home. She looked happy, content, almost ma-
tronly. I wondered if she still drank. Then she told me
she had just gotten back from New York and that she
had seen him. I knew right away who she meant. He
still talks about you, she said. You changed him. He
had told her to have me call him if she ever saw me
again. He gave her a piece of paper with the phone
number, she promised to carry it with her all the time,
and she had it folded up in her purse. She gave it to me.
The handwriting was someone's I had never seen before, but I think it was his. Promise me you'll call him,
she said. I told her I would. Then I went home, and for
a long time I actually thought about it, whether or not
I should call. I felt the wound. It still hurt. Would it
change anything to call him, to hear his voice after all
this time, or would it be like calling a stranger? I was
afraid that by calling him I would start falling all over
again. The sound of his voice would be like a trap
door swinging shut and I would never be free again.
Did he have the power to do that still? I laid the number
on the table and my fingers strayed to the phone and

back again, to the phone, back again. It was a month
later that I finally called him. I thought about all the
people I hadn't found and thought, Let me finish this
at least. A woman answered the phone. I knew she
would. I asked to speak to Mekhti. What if he isn't
here, I thought. I almost hoped he wouldn't be. Then I
could at least say I tried. But who would care except
me? He was so happy to hear from me. He made me
tell him everything that was going on in my life.
College, finals, research projects, possible second au-
thorship on an upcoming paper. He said, I'm glad I
didn't spoil anything for you. He began to tell me
about his life. He loved his family. His younger daughter, Stella, the one on whose birth and baby colds my
happiness had hinged, was just starting kindergarten.
He, Mekhti, was going to night school. And they had
had another baby after he left me, a boy, Alex. We
spoke in English, and that made it all the more strange,
that and his strange accent. When we were together he
had spoken only Persian and there had been no accent. Then his wife must have gone out of the room, or
left, because his buoyant tone changed. His health
was bad, he said. The doctor said his blood pressure
and cholesterol were too high and he was worried
about having a heart attack. He wanted to live to see
his children graduate from high school, get married. (I
remembered how easily frightened he was by colds,
by the flu, by dreams of dying, and I didn't say any-

thing.) He missed me. He thought of me every day. He hadn't been the same person since. I had changed him. Maybe someday I could come to New York, he said. I wanted to cry, Too late, too late. If only you had needed me then, when I needed you. He asked, Do you still love me as much as you did then?

Now that it's too late, I can wonder about what would have happened if I had gotten what I had wanted, gotten him. At the time I couldn't allow myself even to think about it. But when I think about who he was, his lewd jokes, his rough talk, I wonder, would I really have wanted him? Was it really Mekhti I was so crazy about or what he represented? A while ago I read the autobiography of an actress in some magazine. She had met her first husband when she was thirteen and he was twenty-four, married him at sixteen, divorced him by twenty-three. And when people asked her why, she just said, I grew out of him. With Mekhti it would have been like that. Someday, hopefully, I would grow out of him, grow up. I can almost feel sorry for Mekhti, for what he did, because he was an adult when he met me. He would never grow out of me.

Amy Bassan was born in Seattle and grew up in Bellevue, Washington. She matriculated at the University of Washington at age sixteen and graduated with a degree in Russian at nineteen. The following summer she moved to Moscow where she taught English. She returned to the United States after six months to work as a medical interpreter. Many of her clients were members of the Seattle-Bellevue community of Jews from Samarkand, Uzbekistan. When she was twenty she wrote Mekhti in three weeks. At age twenty-one, she married and returned to the University of Washington to study biochemistry and neurobiology. After graduation she moved to a suburb of Chicago to attend medical school. She and her husband have two sons. In addition to writing fiction, she writes music for the piano and acoustic guitar, sculpts and draws.